FOUR EXITS TO HELL

A NOVEL BY
JAMES ALLEN

Copyright © 2019, James Allen

ALL RIGHTS RESERVED

No portion of this literary work may be used or duplicated without the written consent of the owner James Allen.

A Note from The Author

I have tried to recreate events, locales and conversations from my memories of them. In order to maintain their anonymity in some instances I have changed the names of individuals and places, I may have changed some identifying characteristics and details such as physical properties, occupations and places of residence. This is all to ensure the protection and privacy of people involved.

James Allen – Author

Table of Contents

Prologue - page- 6

Brothers- page- 8

Bonnie Disguised as Juliette-page - 12

Meeting the Family- page- 18

New Horizons- page -23

Joe Lane- page- 29

Spinning A Web- page – 33

Suspicions- page – 39

Mike and Tina- page - 45

Burning it Down- page- 49

Pain of Loss and Gain- page – 56

Chasity- page – 61

I Don't Love You-page- 67

Material Things- page – 71

Construction Destruction-page - 78

Return- page – 84

Hello and Goodbye-page - 92

Texas Shopping Spree Comes Home- page – 95

A Set Up- page – 103

The Fall- page – 111

Fishing- page- 117

Running- page – 124

The New Millennium- page – 128

The Long Winter- page – 131

Shots in Ardmore- page- 136

James's Plan-page – 141

Three, Two, One-page – 147

The Day the Angels Wept-page – 151

Dishonor-page – 154

Jess-page - 158

Doppelganger- page – 161

The Last Trip to the Lake- page-165

Back to Dallas- page- 169

River of Tears- page-175

Pulling Back the Veil- page- 178

Mark's Note-page – 182

Dedication-page – 184

About the Author-page - 185

Prologue

Mark sat in the truck, the engine was running, and his heart was hammering with wrath. He didn't know if he should do what he was about to do, he and this man had been friends for years. He had been through hell and back with Gina and this was the last time he would be betrayed by her.

He didn't realize his state of mind wasn't that of a lucid person. All he could think of was hurting this man that had betrayed him, some friend he was. He knew that once this deed was done, he could never go back to freedom or any kind of life, his choice was made, and he wasn't going to back down. He waited and watched the man's house.

Holding the pistol in his lap, a driver pulled into the home's driveway. It was him, Mark only had moments to think about it and he decided that maybe he should let it go, let all of it go. The man exited his vehicle and seen Mark's truck sitting on the curb-side. As he approached Mark's vehicle Mark got out of the truck, still holding the gun.

In an instant it happened, Mark raised the weapon and shot the man in the face. He dropped like a sack of bricks, lying there, legs twitching, arms twitching, the man's blood and shattered face were on the road. Like something from the worst horror movie, only it was real, and that reality crashed on Mark in a millisecond.

Regret, the deepest of regret stabbed at his heart. He fled, if only Gina had never entered his life this wouldn't have ever happened. Lives would never have been lost; her cruelty would be Mark's unraveling.

Brothers

Mark and Mike grew up in Ardmore, a small town with an amazing close - knit family. Mark and Mike were the middle two of four kids total. They also had an older sister and a younger brother. Their parents were very active in their church. They were raised to be respectful young men. All the Allen children were raised with love and discipline. Mark and Mike were your average rowdy boys growing up they played outside, rode their bikes often in Evil Kinevil style, the boys enjoyed catching crawdads in the river.

Their dad owned and operated an upholstery shop in the town where they lived. Mark and his dad were always really close and Mark loved working in the shop with his dad. When Mark was in 6th grade he was persistent in dropping out of school to fully learn the upholstery business with his dad. His mom didn't approve, but in those days the father of the house always made the final decision.

Mark finally won and left school going to work with his dad. It was now a father and son business, a true family business. Mike, who was more of a momma's boy carried on and kept going to school, he wasn't as interested in upholstery as Mark had been. As they got older the two brothers remained close even though they didn't go to school together. They both had pleasant personalities and had lots of friends.

Mike had a ton of friends, he was very outgoing, funny and generally just a good ole boy. People enjoyed being around him, he had a glow that not every person carries. On the weekends when Mark wasn't working, he would hang out with Mike and his friends doing normal teenage stuff. Riding back and forth on the drag was a Friday night must. They would go to the high school parties together, back road, drive and hang out at the lake. Typical southern fun.

To the world they were your average teenagers and that's because they were. As the years went on though their dad was getting older and wanted to spend more time near the lake, fishing and slowing down a little he was ready for his time after raising a family. Since Mark was excelling at auto upholstery their dad decided it was time to move to a smaller town near Kingston. They settled in nicely, they lived just walking distance from the lake. The entire family enjoyed being near the lake, it was peaceful. Mark and Mike quickly made new friends and felt at home.

Their dad did upholstery out of a small shop on the family property. Mark felt that it was a little too slow paced for him and he wanted something more. He decided he wanted to put his new trade to good use and have a big shop of his own. One weekend he and Mike drove to Durant, a nearby town to hang out with some new friends that Mike made at school. Mark spotted a vacant building on the main street that had a 'for lease' sign in the window. He thought to himself he could turn that into an upholstery shop and really have his own business.

He quickly turned his truck at the next street, Mike had no idea what Mark was up to. Mike asked Mark,

"I thought we were going to get tacos?"

Mark laughed and said "just a minute I wanna look at something."

Mark pulled into the empty parking lot, throwing the truck in park, he left his door open and ran up to the sign. He pulled an ink pen out and began writing the number on his hand. His heart was beating with hope.

Later that night Mark kept day dreaming about starting his very own shop. The very next day he called the number, an older man's voice said "hello", with excitement in his voice Mark said

"I am calling about the vacant building on Main Street that you have for lease."

The man said that it was still available and would be glad to show it to him. Mark asked him how much it was and the gentleman told him $500 per month. Mark was grinning from ear to ear and set the appointment to see it the next day. Mark told Mike about it but Mike told him he was crazy and that he wasn't old enough to have his own shop. Mark could barely sleep that night thinking about all the possibilities.

The next day Mark woke up and went to his appointment to see the building. It was a great day! Barely eighteen – years- old and he now had his own building! Mark went home excited telling his family the excellent news. Throughout the week Mark would gather material and take it to the building to set up his new shop. His dad helped him in getting supplies and ordered him a brand - new sign for the building. It was stunning and made the business feel truly alive. It had a white back ground and bold red letters that read:

"MARK'S UPHOLSTERY"

In a matter of 24 hours Mark now had his own business! As the months went on, Mark's new business was a growing success! In Mark's downtime He began doing body work on his own truck, he was self - taught and decided to start adding auto body to the list of services that he offered at his shop. Mike would come up on the weekends and help Mark he enjoyed learning from his older brother.

Bonnie Disguised as Juliette

Gina was a high school senior, pretty and intelligent. Charismatic is one way to describe her, she had plenty of charm. People were drawn to her she was fun, bubbly, and she had eyes for Mark. Mark and Gina had met at a party a couple weeks before.

Gina was there to have a dent fixed, her passenger side door was practically caved in. She really wasn't supposed to be driving, Gina had received a driving while intoxicated charge. She was a free – spirited young lady and had made her way around the party circuit. She didn't tell Mark how she had dented the car. Luckily, she had side swiped a tree and not a family.

Mark was surprised to see her, he hadn't laid eyes on her since the party, but he hadn't forgotten her. She was after all, unforgettable. Gina was the type of woman that men did not easily forget. With her blonde hair, blue eyes and legs for days. Mark wasn't highly experienced with women; he wasn't nearly as experienced as her.

Mark was completely captivated by her looks and her outgoing personality. Gina was equally head over heels for him, she hadn't happened into his shop by accident. One of her friends at the party had mentioned that Mark was already a go getter. Gina liked that, she liked that he was only a year older than her and he was a business man. The idea of having him was alluring to her.

"Hey there you're Gina, right?" Mark asked her, a little shyly.

"Yeah, and you're Mark? I saw you like, a week or two ago at a party, didn't I?" Gina asked, in a sweet voice.

"Yeah, yeah um…I was there. I saw you too. You were pretty busy though. There was a lot of dancing going on. I'm pretty sure you out drank me." Mark said with a sly grin this time.

"I am so embarrassed about that! I did have a few too many, but it was all in good fun. I am glad I remembered you though." Gina said to him with a sparkle in her blue eyes. She shifted one foot to the other.

"I am glad you did too, I don't really know many people here in town yet besides customers." He said.

"Oh, so, you are new around here then? I knew we didn't go to school together. So, where are you from?" she asked.

"I'm from Ardmore, that's where I grew up my family just recently moved here. I'm just keeping on with the family business." He replied as he tucked his dirty shop rag in his back pocket.

"That's really cool, I haven't known anyone our age that has ever had their own business. I mean, most guys around here end up working in the oil fields or finding factory work. I'm impressed!"

Gina was talking with enthusiasm. She was truly impressed by his accomplishments.

Gina and Mark talked back and forth until her ride arrived. As she was leaving Mark watched the back of the car as it pulled out and felt his heart hammering against his rib cage. Gina was looking out the windshield, her heart hammering the same as Mark's.

Mark was a silent type and that was more conversation than he had held in a while. He felt something unfamiliar to him, he had never been in love, but this meeting had left his head and heart racing. Gina was feeling the same tug on her heart. They were both already in love, the kind of love that happens on the big screen or romantic novels. They were like magnets that couldn't be pulled apart and this day would start the beginning of many that they would spend together. These two were the couple to be envied, and most did, everyone dreams of an instantaneous connection. Mark and Gina had it.

Gina showed up the next day, she knew her car wouldn't be fixed yet, but she wanted Mark's attention. She wanted him to date her so bad it was driving her mad. Mark was genuinely excited to see her; he couldn't believe his luck that this woman liked him. He could tell she was into him, but he had no idea how much. Gina felt the same, she could tell he was interested, and she decided to act on it. She brought up that maybe they should go on a date.

Mark agreed, trying to maintain his masculine composure. On the inside though, he was lit up like a Christmas tree.

Gina was tired of waiting for Mark to ask her out so she took matters into her own hands. She asked him if he would like to go out with her to the local burger joint, the one where she worked. Mark agreed without hesitation, he kind of wished he had asked her first but that was the type of girl Gina was, always going after what she wanted.

Mark noticed that the men stared at her like a steak, he didn't like it, but he decided not to say anything since it was their first date. The night had been fun and innocent enough, some of her friends were flirting with Mark but he shrugged them off. He wasn't rude, he was clearly not participating with the flirty girls though. They had a really good time they visited and found one another's company to be very interesting. Mark felt comfortable with Gina she had a way of doing that with men.

At Mark's house they sat on the couch together, talking about their goals in life and their child-hoods, etc.… Mark had a bottle of whiskey in the cabinet and they drank some while they talked. Before long, talking turned into nuzzling and then kissing. They both felt the electricity pulsating between them. There was no going back for either of them, in the starry-eyed gaze they shared they couldn't have known it, but they would be the modern-day

Bonnie and Clyde. In that house began a love that would bring them to their knees. A love that no one else could fathom.

When they awoke the next morning, they lay there looking at one another, Gina was smiling gently and stroking the side of Mark's cheek. He felt like they were the only two people on the planet. He felt like she was in orbit around him, he felt special, more than special. Mark felt singular in her eyes. The way she looked at him made him know that he was the only man for her. Gina could see the same radiating from Mark.

Gina had to go, she had told her mom that she was staying the night with her friend Katie and had to check in at home. Before she left the two of them made plans for the next date. As the week went on, Gina in school day dreaming about Mark and Mark at work day dreaming about Gina the weekend was finally here. Mark went to pick Gina up and they hung out with some of her friends at the lake.

They spent the entire weekend together; he went to the shop long enough to make sure his guys had everything going smoothly and the rest of his time was spent with her. They stayed tucked away in his house, talking about their dreams, he would tell her his dreams of expansion and someday working on classic cars and it was perfection because their dreams seemed to align. Everything he wanted; she wanted the same.

They fit together like pieces of a jig saw puzzle in Mark's mind. Before the weekend was over and they had to face the real world again, they hastily decided to move in together.

Gina had brought up the fact that she was about to graduate and she never wanted to spend a moment away from him. Mark's life could not have been any better now. He had it all, his business and an unexpected, ravenous love. Regardless of how happy he was it still surprised him when Gina suggested that she start living there.

Things were moving so fast Mark didn't have time to get his bearings but he knew he wanted her, so naturally he agreed. Gina began moving her things in while Mark worked. Despite himself Mark was one happy guy when he saw all of Gina's things in his… now their home. He knew she was the one, his Juliette.

Meeting the Family

Mark decided it was time to introduce Gina to his family. This was a big deal; he hadn't ever brought someone home to meet his folks and siblings. He had mentioned to his dad that he had been on a few dates but nothing more. When they arrived the house was empty, he hadn't called ahead. He and Gina decided to wait on the front porch of his parent's home.

They waited and talked for a while then innocent kissing turned into full on indecent making out. They didn't care who could see them by this point, and his parents pulled in the driveway to witness this with his little brother in the backseat of the car. Mark's mom and dad were not impressed by the public display that was playing out on their porch.

Mrs. Allen looked to her husband and stated, "this girl is going to be trouble."

It wasn't that they weren't happy for their son, but they did not tolerate this kind of behavior. Mark knew this, he and Gina turned down the heat as his parents and brother walked up the front porch steps.

"Mom, Dad, this is Gina. Gina, this is my folks" before he could say anything else Mr. and Mrs. Allen had taken their young son in the house.

Mark followed behind them and looked at Gina apologetically. They should have been the ones apologizing for the show they were putting on for the neighborhood. The incident would be let go, the Allen's weren't going to hold a grudge against their son, they had just raised him better than to act like that. Mark's feelings for Gina were over riding his senses though, and he did feel bad for the steamy make out session on his parent's porch. He announced that they were moving in together, both of his parents looked at him with narrowed eyes.

"It's a little soon, don't you think son?" Mrs. Allen asked.

"Not at all, we love each other, I know it seems fast, but we want to be together." Mark said firmly to his mom.

Mrs. Allen looked over at Gina with disapproval on her face. She felt they were moving incredibly fast; she didn't want to see her love – struck son end up with a broken heart. However, she, also knew that Mark was going to do as he pleased. Mike their second oldest son had just married his high school sweet heart, Tina. Mark had yet to introduce Gina to them. He and Mike had talked though, and Mike did know about this rapid turn of events in his brother's life. Gina didn't speak much to Marks parents. She seemed to have a sense of superiority that was only picked up on by Mark's mom.

After they had left Mark was spewing apologies to Gina, he tried telling her they were just strict. Gina wasn't really listening to what he was saying. She was too busy telling him how rude and absurd their 'morals' were. Mark understood she was upset but he wasn't particularly fond of her calling his parents' names. He finally chalked it up to their differences in how they had been raised.

"Your mom doesn't like me. I could see that much!" Gina had said vehemently to Mark.

"It's not about liking you, she's just old fashioned." Mark responded.

"Pfft, Ok, well she can be *old fashioned* all she wants but I know she didn't like me." Gina was being hot headed.

"Look, it doesn't matter, what matters is how I think of you, and how you think of me, right?" Mark said as he brought her into a hug.

Gina stubbornly agreed with Mark, she couldn't stand not to be liked and she wasn't used to not being the center of attention. This was her first real relationship too and she had expected the red – carpet treatment like she was used to getting from her friends and family. Mark's family held higher standards than what she was used to dealing with. Gina had let her sense of entitlement slip just a small fraction, but Mark hadn't noticed. Gina's monster in her pocket didn't go unnoticed by Mrs. Allen though.

The next day Mark and Gina were going to be meeting up with Mike and his wife. They were more laid back, naturally. They were all close to the same age and they were brothers not one another's keeper. Tina and Gina hung out in the kitchen for a bit catching up, the two women had gone to school together. They made some side dishes to go with the BBQ, the guys were in the back-yard cooking. Mark asked Mike what he thought about Gina, Mike just smiled at his brother and said to him that she seemed like a 'damn fine woman,' she was easy on the eyes too. Mark was happy to hear his brother's approval after the fiasco at mom and dad's house.

Mark told Mike what had happened, and Mike snickered at him.

"Well you know how they are, don't act so surprised that they weren't their friendliest." Mike told him.

"Yeah but now she thinks mom hates her and it's all I keep hearing about. I tried telling her mom doesn't hate her, they're just old fashioned." Mark responded.

"Yeah, they are, and you know that. Don't worry man, mom will come around, she always does." Mike assured his brother.

The girls came out with the side dishes and set the picnic table for dinner. Ice cold beer and BBQ, nothing better than that on a nice summer night. The four of them visited for several hours, drinking beer and cutting up. It was a good time, Gina felt welcomed and she really liked Mike, he was such a nice guy. She liked Tina too, but Gina had always found it easier to talk to guys, they weren't as judgmental as other females. Mike thought his brother had done good for himself. The four were in their primes, life was just getting interesting.

New Horizons

The couple had been together for over a year now and Mark was getting more and more work. He was very proud of what he had achieved with his business. He had started dabbling with buying and selling cars as well. With upholstery, auto body, and mechanics under his belt, naturally he began selling vehicles.

Mark and Gina couldn't have been happier, it was a fairy tale come true for them. They were young, in love, and enjoying life. Gina worked part time at the shop helping keep the office in order. Mark was proving to be quite the business man. He was smart, and he was making good financial decisions that were keeping the pair comfortable. Gina didn't want for anything, Mark provided her with everything she asked for and then some. He lavished her with gifts and every spare moment of his time.

As time went on Gina eventually starting working full time at the shop and was putting in more and more effort into helping make the business an even larger success. Gina now had full access to everything; the bank account, and every minute detail of how the business operated. Things went like that for another year and it was seemingly perfect.

Mark was in high demand in Durant and other surrounding towns. He could take an old mangled car and turn it back into what it looked like when it had been new sitting on a lot. His work was truly impeccable, he had a God given talent. His abilities didn't go unnoticed by people in need of the best work.

One of the things Mark loved was spending time with his family. Gina felt that too much time was spent going over to the Allen's home for dinner. However, Mark's parents had decided that they were going to move back to Ardmore. Gina felt relieved since they wouldn't be so close, she wanted all of the attention from Mark on her, but it wasn't. Mark loved his family and he and Gina had been raised completely different in regards of how family worked as a unit.

Mark and his dad had always been close so the couple still went to Ardmore fairly often to visit Mark's mom and dad. Mark and Gina didn't spend very much time with Gina's parents, Gina was always embarrassed of her mother the bar tender, because she didn't have a very nice house and drove an old beat up car. Gina measured success by material things such as name brand clothes, new cars, big houses, not by character, values or good health. Unfortunately, Mark was slow to catching on to the actual reasons they stayed away.

Had he known he would have encouraged more visits to see her parents. He was a firm believer in family and her reasoning would have hurt his heart. Mark loved her to no end though, and since she was firm on not seeing her family much he didn't push.

As family goes, they were all about to receive some fantastic news though!

Mike and Tina were pregnant! Mike was going to be a daddy! With this unexpected news the couple decided that they too would move to Ardmore. There was more opportunity for them there. As a bonus they would be near family during this special time in their lives.

Gina quickly realized that she did not have Mark's full attention because they found themselves in Ardmore every free moment visiting Mark's family. Gina, in her selfishness did not see that she was Mark's entire world. Mark spoiled Gina and everything that he did was for her happiness. Being successful wasn't necessarily all about him being a big shot business owner anymore. Gina wasn't capable of seeing that though, she wasn't appreciative she was expectant.

Gina had dreamed of moving out of Mark's small trailer house and she had brought it up multiple times that they needed a *real* home, one that they could purchase together, as a couple. Mark always avoided the subject because he was comfortable where they were at.

Gina schemed on how to get the fancy home she so desired. She planted the idea that they should buy a house in Ardmore, that way they could be close to his family. As another catalyst to her plan she mentioned how they could grow the business even more.

Gina was right in that regard; Ardmore was bigger and with Mark's talents he could make a hell of a lot more money. Mark was sold on the idea, he told Gina to start looking! The very next day Gina starting scouting out houses that were for sale. Her heart soared and her happiness made Mark happy.

The house hunt didn't go as planned for Gina, oh she found plenty of houses that she wanted and could see herself in. Every time she showed Mark a house, he would tell her that they were way out of their price range. Mark told Gina that she needed to be practical when looking for a house. Something that they could afford and live comfortably in without incurring financial hardship. Gina would pout and give Mark the cold shoulder, she would push him away and make him feel like shit. She would make Mark feel like he wasn't providing good enough for them. Gina knew exactly how to play on Mark's sympathies.

After looking at house after house and them not being able to decide Mark finally found 'the house' It was a small 2 - bedroom house, priced less than what he wanted to spend. That was even better in his book! It was in a quiet neighborhood, it had a big garage which he loved, all together the house was cozy and comfortable, he was finally excited! He called his parents to come and look at it too he wanted to share his and Gina's find with them. His parents agreed that it would be a perfect home for them to start out in! Marks mom loved the house, she told him that if he didn't buy it, she would! Mark was the one who finally made a decision for them and he stood by it, he was proud of his first house.

Gina thought it was ridiculous that Mark would even consider such a small house. She was furious that she was not going to be able to get her way. Mark asked her how they could afford the house she wanted? It was completely out of their price range. She told him that if he would work harder, they could have gotten the one she wanted.

She spat her words at him like venom from a cobra. Gina made Mark feel like a total failure. However, after a few days of bickering Mark put his foot down and decided that was the house that they were going to buy. Gina was going to have to deal with it, he worked his ass off for her and this was the most ungrateful he had ever seen her.

As they were getting settled into their first home it was now time to find a building to rent for Mark to start his business in. That small obstacle didn't take long at all, he found a cheap building that would work just fine. Mark didn't really need big flashy things to make him happy, he liked the simple things in life.

All was good, they got the business transitioned to Ardmore and the business steadily picked back up. Everyday Gina made snide remarks about how the new house wasn't big enough for them, and how it was not working for them. Mark started to think in the back of his mind that Gina was turning into someone that he didn't know. Mark didn't realize that Gina had always been this way, she had been really good at hiding her true nature to get the things that she wanted.

Since Mark was originally from Ardmore he quickly reconnected with old friends, and Gina made new friends quickly. Aside from Gina's constant nagging about not having nicer things, the couple had settled in and felt like they were at home. Gina would hang out with her new girlfriends, she spent time with Tina, and have the occasional girl's night out.

As the months went by, her girl's nights would turn into over nights. This started causing a huge rift between the couple. Gina would apologize, but she would make Mark feel bad about her 'not' having a life. She would claim that Mark didn't want her to have fun, and live her life her way.

Joe Lane

The new location for the shop was doing great, as demand grew, Mark new he was going to need hire someone. Mark delegated the task to Gina, he just required that they have body knowledge, and be dependable. Gina went through applications and interviewed a few people before she got to Joe Lane. Joe was eighteen, and cars were basically his life. The kid seemed intelligent enough and carried a dependable air about him. Gina liked him, but not because of what he could do for the shop, she saw potential in what he could do for her.

Mark and Joe ended up working good together, their work was the finest in their part of Oklahoma. As the months went by, Gina spoke to Joe often, and asked him some fairly personal questions. She barely had any respect for boundaries and since she was his boss, she felt it was ok to pry into his life. Gina learned that Joe didn't have any family left to speak of and the family he did have didn't live anywhere near Oklahoma.

Gina liked the sound of that, she was always plotting in the back of her mind. She figured she could find good use in Joe other than being a regular employee. Since he had been drifting around doing odd jobs to support himself until he had been hired by her, she knew she could use him without his family being an issue. Joe opened up to her because she was easy to talk to and he felt he owed her big time for his position at the lot.

Joe didn't mind opening up to Gina, she made him feel safe. He didn't understand why, he just felt like she really cared about his well-being. Joe hadn't had anyone in his life make him feel that way for a very long time.

Joe enjoyed their alone time when Mark was out of the shop and Gina could see it in his eyes when he spoke to her. She had always been able to see the weakness in men. Gina had been raised very different than Mark and it was slowly starting to show. The changes weren't obvious to anyone but Gina, she could feel herself start to crave her old way of life. She wasn't about to part with Mark though, so she tried to curb her appetite for the party life.

She would hang out with her girlfriends, and she and Mark would spend time with Mike and Tina. As Mark's businesses became more profitable there was one thing she couldn't hide and that was her love of money and her desire for the finer things.

Before long Gina demanded a newer car, she claimed she needed something that fit her success. It wasn't her success though, it was Mark's. Without him she had nothing, he was the one with success but he didn't mind sharing with her. She was constantly shopping, buying new clothes every day and going to get her hair done regularly. Gina always had the finest manicures and pedicures her wardrobe was impeccable. She always looked like a high - class citizen with the jewelry she would buy for herself along with everything else she could think of. Gina had become a shopping fanatic. She was always spending money on frivolous things that they didn't need. New furniture when she grew tired of looking at what she had purchased the previous month. New décor to keep up with the latest home trends. Gina's greedy pit knew no bounds.

Mark would confront her about her insane spending but she would spew word vomit at him that always ended up making him feel less than a good man. He tried to maintain his integrity but she slowly chipped away at him and he loved her to no end so he allowed her outrageous spending to continue.

Joe was always there ready with the compliments that Gina thrived on from others. It didn't matter who it was but she did particularly love being complimented by the opposite sex and if she caught the faintest hint of jealousy from another woman, she reveled in it. Gina at her core was cruel but the depths of her cruelty weren't even obvious to her yet. Gina by her nature was simply mean and out for herself and instant gratification.

Joe was enamored with her though, he felt that this woman hung the moon and stars. He would do anything for her, and he did. When Gina approached him about spying on Mark for her, he eagerly agreed. She didn't reveal her true intentions to Joe for her reason of wanting him to spy. She wasn't worried that he was being a run about, rather she wanted to know his location at all times so she could carry on with whatever she wanted to get into.

Joe was a pawn to her, a disposable piece of a chess board. He was a great employee though. Mark was always happy with his work. Joe was a gift that he needed due to the rise in business. Mark wasn't aware that Joe was reporting all of his activity to Gina, if he had it would not have been pleasant for Gina or Joe.

Joe did as Gina asked and each time, she asked something of him he felt more needed by her. He thrived on the feeling of being needed by this woman he perceived as perfect and caring. His feelings would get away from him sometimes and he would carefully reign them in. He didn't want Gina to know that he had fallen head over heels for her, being her lap dog was good enough for him for now.

Gina always slipped extra bills in his pay for his services regarding being Mark's secret babysitter. Someone that Mark looked at as a colleague and friend was really someone he couldn't trust and he had no clue. The situation on the surface was seemingly perfect but under the still water there was an under tow that could suck them all under if they were caught in the current.

<u>Spinning A Web</u>

Gina knew that she had Mark wrapped around not just one but all of her fingers. She wasn't about to let him go, she had spent her child – hood hoping and praying for a prince and that is what she had in Mark. Someone to take care of her. The romantic aspect of their relationship was fizzled out to her. Gina had always been the party girl, the center of male affections. The only man that she had been able to ensnare for this long was Mark. That was because he truly loved her, he would do anything to make her happy. There had been guys in the past, but she had been a passing thing. She had never met anyone like Mark, he was handsome, kind, and financially stable at their young age. Gina knew she had hit the jack pot. She wasn't about to give that up.

Mark's questions about her whereabouts and what she had been doing the previous night were not far from her thoughts. She knew she didn't want to quit her personal activities, but she couldn't risk losing Mark. Gina spent the next couple weeks cooking up a scheme to have her cake and eat it to. While she was dreaming up a plan, she walked a straight line, making sure to keep him happy, she didn't want to muck up what she had. Mark didn't know it, but he had fallen victim to a woman with a very sick and twisted mind. Gina had managed to keep herself under control for three years now, but she couldn't maintain. She wasn't changed, his love for her could not change what she really was. Gina carried a darkness within her that the brightest light couldn't penetrate.

Mark and Joe were working on a wrecked car, a good insurance job and Gina was sitting in the office. It was a typical day of work, at least that is what the guys thought. Mark had no idea that Gina was getting ready to do something incredibly unconscionable to him. All for the sake of her maintaining her lifestyle away from his eye shot. The training that she had learned growing up was about to come in handy, she smiled to herself as she thought of how perfect her plan was.

If Gina knew anything it was how her mother had taught her to use her body to get what she wanted from men. She knew how to bend over just so, it didn't look entirely on purpose. Gina knew how to show just enough cleavage, yes, she had been taught by the best, her mom had duplicated a perfect copy of her younger self.

It was after work and Joe came into the office to collect his paycheck. He sat across her desk as she wrote out a check for the week, as she handed it to him, she slid her fingers ever so lightly across his. Joe felt an electrical surge run through his body. He had blushed slightly, and Gina noticed before he ducked his head down and mumbled a 'thanks'.

"Joe, ya know I think you have done great work here for us. I think you deserve something special for all your hard work." Gina said to him with a mischievous smile on her lips.

"Really?" Joe asked, noticing her smile.

"Yes, I think you and me should have drinks one night soon." Gina said, now smiling and twirling the end of her blonde hair.

"Ok, hanging out with you guys again would be fun." Joe said, he too had a mischievous smile.

"No, just us. Alone." Gina said, glancing at the office door, making sure Mark wasn't headed inside.

"I think I would like that very much. When would you like to have drinks?" Joe replied.

"Next Saturday, and dress nice. I want to take you somewhere special." Gina said now with zero playfulness.

"Yes ma'am, you are the boss." Joe said to her. He could feel his pulse quicken at the thought of being alone with her.

Gina smiled and nodded, they agreed for the following Saturday, and she told him to keep it to himself. This was their secret, she told him that Mark wouldn't approve. He knew that but he played along like it was innocent enough. He leaned forward, tapped the desk like he wanted to say something else but instead he looked to his side and stood up. Joe went out of the office and it had been settled. He knew he had just agreed to a rendezvous with Mark's girlfriend. He felt a little guilty but not much.

Gina was proud of her accomplishment; she would do what needed done. Then Joe would be at her disposal, she needed him in ways that only she knew. It wasn't a magical chemistry or an unplanned scandal. Gina knew exactly what she was doing. After their night together, Joe would be hers. Joe would have to do what she said or face Mark's wrath. This was how she was going to get her cake and eat it too.

The following week at work was stressful to say the least, Joe's anticipation of meeting with Gina preoccupied him. Mark had to keep either fixing his mistakes or correcting him verbally. Mark didn't know what had gotten into Joe, he was normally a very cool, level headed, and on spot with his work kind of guy. Mark asked him what the issue was, and Joe stammered on about some nonsense regarding one of his distant relatives.

"Well do you need some time off?" Mark asked.

"No, no, it's good, I'm just worried about my uh aunt. I think she will be ok." Joe was a bad liar.

"Alright, if you're sure. I don't mind giving you a week off." Mark offered.

"Nah man, I can't afford to lose the pay. It will be alright. I'll get my shit together." Joe said.

Mark was fine with his answer but oblivious to the obvious lie he was being fed; Mark was trusting to a fault. He would have never imagined Gina and Joe betraying him.

Gina walked out to the garage to see what the guys were up to; she was bored of sitting in the office. Plus, she thought it would be fun to ruffle Joe's feathers. She had a jean skirt, and tight top that left little to the imagination. Joe hadn't been with a woman in a long time and she definitely aroused him. Mark walked over to her slipping his hand around her waist and pulled her in for a kiss.

"You're gonna get me all dirty." She said in a teasing tone.

"You are beautiful, have I told you that lately?" Mark asked jokingly with a glimmer in his eye.

"No, I don't think so." Gina said looking up at him with a big grin on her face.

"Baby, you are beautiful." Mark kissed Gina.

Joe watched from the other side of the car they were working on and tried to ignore the exchange. He felt excitement at the prospect of holding Gina in his arms. He hoped that she would end up being his woman and they could leave together. Joe had many ideas and fantasies regarding Gina and himself. He liked Mark, but he didn't feel loyalty towards him, all he could think about was Gina.

The weekend was rapidly approaching, and Gina was looking forward to the night with Joe, after they were together, she felt like she would own him. He would do whatever she wanted; she couldn't get enough of having men in her pockets. Gina's fiendish side couldn't be suppressed any longer. She knew that men were valuable, the right kind of men. She wouldn't mess around with anyone that couldn't be valuable to her in some way. Mark was the longest relationship she had ever had but her appetite had grown, not just for the touch of someone different but for the feeling of power over another life.

Joe met her at the hotel they had agreed on, they stayed in the room to keep from being seen by prying eyes. Gina didn't want it getting around Ardmore that she was fooling around with the help. Gina charmed Joe with her smile and tinkling laughter, she acted like he was the most interesting person she had ever met. They spent the night together and Joe was caught in her web. He didn't know that he was a pawn, he thought Gina really had feelings for him.

He would do anything for this woman, she was the only woman who had ever treated him like he really was something special. Joe was stupid, he allowed himself to become a fly, a mere insect that would be consumed gradually by the spider. When daylight broke Gina left. She had already showered and rid herself of another man's scent. Joe still slept soundly in the bed they had practically destroyed with their lust. When Gina arrived home, Mark sat waiting on the front porch, smelling of whiskey and fury.

Suspicions

Mark watched as Gina pulled in the driveway in her new Camaro that he bought her for her birthday, he was furious. He thought they had put all of this behind them. Mark had always been soft with Gina but now the alcohol was fueling his anger. He had made it clear to her that the late nights and disappearing acts were not going to continue. He felt himself bubbling over with anger. Despite the red that he was seeing, he softened a little when she exited the car smiling at him with a big grin.

"Hey babe! I had so much fun with the girls!" Gina said as she approached the porch.

"Where have you been Gina?"

"I just said I had fun with the girls so, that would mean I was with the girls." Gina said rolling her eyes.

"I thought we agreed no more mysterious nights out. No more of you just taking off and doing whatever you want." Mark said with a bite in his voice.

"Mark, I'm young, you knew how I was when we got together. I have stayed under your thumb ever since we met! I will do what I want, or I will leave. You decide." She challenged Mark with a shrug of her shoulders.

"Leave" Mark said with coldness.

"You don't mean that." She said with a weak laugh.

"Yes, I do. Get your shit and get out." Mark said through gritted teeth.

"Fine, you will regret this. I am the only woman who will put up with the way you work, ignoring your relationship. Good luck finding another woman who will stick by your side!" Gina yelled, and stomped past him slamming the front door.

Gina was packing a bag, throwing this and that in it. She was furious, she knew he would be mad, but she never thought he would kick her out. Mark walked in, he sat down on the side of the bed with his back away from her. The words she said stung him, but he didn't feel like he ignored her, hell, they worked together day in and out. He couldn't understand why she felt neglected. In reality, she wasn't neglected but she knew how to slice with her words. Gina walked past him and out of the house. He could hear her car come to life and fade away.

Gina knocked on Mike and Tina's door. Mike answered; the knocking had woken him up. He looked at Gina with surprise.

"What are you doing here?" He asked.

"Mark was drunk and kicked me out." Gina said, only telling half the truth. The part that made her look like the victim.

"That's a damn shame, come on in. You look tired, I'll get you a blanket and pillow." Mike said as he let her in.

"That doesn't sound like Mark, I wonder what got in to him?" Mike asked.

"He was mad because I went out with my girlfriends last night, I told him I would be out, but I guess he drank so much he forgot." Gina told Mike without a hint of lying. She added a frown for good measure.

Mike shook his head from side to side slowly. He fetched her a pillow and blanket. Gina made the couch to sleep, Mike decided to stay awake, he went to put on the coffee. Mike knew what she was saying didn't sound like his brother but from the looks of her she had a long night. He couldn't decide what was going on. Tina got up a couple hours later, she walked into the kitchen following the aroma of coffee. She saw her husband sitting at the kitchen table sipping coffee and holding their son.

"Hey Hun, what's Gina doing on the couch?" Tina asked.

"She says Mark got drunk and kicked her out." Mike responded not looking up from the paper.

"That doesn't sound right, have they been having problems?" Tina asked.

Mike looked up at his wife while she got a cup from the cabinet. "I have no idea, me and Mark don't talk about that kind of stuff much."

"I hope they can work it out, they have been together for what, three years now?" Tina asked.

"Yeah, something like that." Mike said.

Mike and Tina had been having their own issues. They weren't in the best situation to be dealing with Mark and Gina's issues. Mike wasn't going to turn her away though. He had always had a soft spot for Gina, he didn't realize it but so did every other man. He wouldn't have been surprised though, she was easy on the eyes and had a sexy personality in his opinion. Mike liked her a little more than he should, he kept that to himself though.

Gina had always been able to tell he liked her; she had a sense for these things. She knew she had the goods and she would use her feminine prowess to her advantage when she needed. Gina was like the mythical siren; her song would bring the men in only to kill them later. She had ruined a few hearts already. Gina didn't go to Mike and Tina's because she had nowhere else to go, she knew it would drive Mark crazy.

Mark had gone back onto the porch of their house. He watched the morning song birds through a drunken haze. He didn't know if he believed her story of being out with girls. She hadn't done anything to make him believe otherwise, but he had a feeling that she wasn't being honest. A woman like her didn't go out and not have to deal with the advances of men. He wondered if she stayed away from men, he knew she had a huge sexual appetite.

Mark tried to make heads or tails of what she had meant by him ignoring her and the other stuff she had rambled at him. He knew he had always made sure she had everything she wanted. Mark didn't want to lose her, not really. He decided to go to bed and sleep off the alcohol, he would think about it with a sober mind.

Gina woke up late that evening, Mike and Tina had left her a note saying they would be back soon and if she left to lock the door. She had no intentions of going anywhere for the time being. She wasn't sure how long they would let her stay, but she wasn't going to stray too far from Mark. She knew he would let her come home.

Gina, the real Gina, was now coming into full swing, she wouldn't let anything stand between her and what she wanted. What she wanted was Mark, what Mark owned, and what Mark could still provide for her. She picked up the phone and dialed the number to her house. In her mind it was hers not theirs. The phone rang a few times until a groggy Mark answered.

"Hello." He said gruffly.

"Hey Baby, I'm sorry about this morning and last night." Gina lied. "Can I come home and us talk about this?" She asked.

There was a silence …

"Mark?" She asked.

"Whatever, I guess. Where are you?" He asked.

"Mike and Tina's house."

"Why did you go there?" He asked.

"They have always been nice to me." Gina said in a whiny sort of kiddie voice.

"Just, come home Gina. We'll talk." Mark hung up.

Gina smiled to herself, she knew she was going to win this round. She would come out the victor and she was proud. She would convince him that he was overthinking things, and she would call her girlfriends for an alibi. Gina had all of her bases covered. By staying at Mike and Tina's it showed that she has feelings for his family. Her friends would vouch for her that they had all been at the bar. Lastly, Joe would never say a word, she would see him the next day at work and make sure of it. She was feeling pretty happy with herself.

Mike and Tina

Mike and Tina had been on the rocks for a few months now. They had their child and everything should have been perfect. It wasn't perfect though. She didn't understand the change in her husband. Tina thought that they had a great marriage, they had been high school sweethearts and in her mind this kind of thing wouldn't happen. They had a son together and they were supposed to be happy. Mike had changed though, she didn't know how to fix it, she couldn't fix it if she didn't know what the issue was.

Tina's best friend who was also named Tina tried to be there as much as possible for her friend. They were differentiated by Big Tina, being Mike's wife and Little Tina being the best friend. Little Tina was always at their house, Mike acted irritated by her ever presence. He felt like he couldn't get a moments peace with the two women always having their hen parties. Big Tina had decided she didn't care if her friend being at their home was annoying to him or not. She was fed up with the distance he had put between them.

Little Tina was concerned for her friend's marriage, she had lost a husband to a car accident. His breaks had stopped working, the report said they had been cut. Everyone in Ardmore pointed their finger at her, she did inherit a great deal of money from his death, but she was aghast that she would be blamed. They never found out who had done it, she figured it was some kid who didn't understand the finality of death. So, now she would be here for her friend she didn't have anything else to do, she was widowed and secretly she kind of enjoyed their drama. It was entertaining to her since she didn't have anything else going on and she was thought to be a black widow. Big Tina had been the only person in the town that hadn't turned their back or shifted their gaze away from her. Big Tina had never accused her, and she appreciated that in Big Tina.

Mike was in the living room trying to watch the T.V. and he could hear the women in the kitchen yammering away. He didn't say anything to them, he acted like he didn't like Little Tina being there so much but in honesty he liked her. To him she was beautiful, friendly, and everything he wanted. Little Tina could pick up on the vibe, but Big Tina was oblivious to their subtle flirtation. Mike wanted her, when his wife wasn't around, and it was just the two of them he could feel his heart quicken, and she would blush for no obvious reason. There was a magnetic attraction, but they hadn't acted on it.

Big Tina and Little Tina seemed to always be together, his and Little Tina's moments alone were very few. As he sat there watching the program, but not really watching it he made a choice. Mike walked in the kitchen and asked the ladies if they would be up for drinks since their son was at his grandma's house. Both women eagerly agreed, it sounded fun and since it was his idea Big Tina was hopeful that he was coming around.

The trio loaded into Mikes truck and went to the liquor store. "Pick your poison ladies." Mike told them when they walked in the shop.

Big Tina and Little Tina walked around the store for a few minutes, they had decided on tequila, they wanted to make margaritas. Mike joked with them about that being a girly drink and opted for a bottle of Crown. They got back to the house and the women started making margaritas, Mike poured him a Crown and coke.

Everyone was loosened up after an hour and they decided to play spades. Mike positioned himself between the two women. They played several hands, laughed and joked. Big Tina was getting tired though, she told the other two she was going to call it a night. Little Tina groaned, and Mike stayed quiet. After his wife had gone to bed Mike and Little Tina stayed awake talking.

He drunkenly confided in her that he wasn't happy anymore. He told her he felt he married too young and he had never been with another woman. Rather that was true or not was anyone's guess. Little Tina listened to him, she had listened to her friend so, why not listen to Mike? She did like him, and she had always found him attractive. She liked being the shoulder he needed.

"Have you told Tina how you feel? Because she thinks you just hate her." Little Tina said.

"Nah, I don't know how to tell her I don't love her anymore." Mike said.

"If you don't love her then you need to leave." Little Tina said as she put her hand on top of his.

Electricity moved in the air between them. For the first time Mike looked at Little Tina, really looked at her. He was surprised that he hadn't noticed her beauty before. They left their hands like that, hers sitting atop his.

After a few moments Mike cleared his throat breaking the trance. Little Tina moved her hand from his. Mike stood up and offered his hand down to Little Tina. She took it and stood. They were now face to face, Mike closed the gap between them and kissed her. She didn't stop him. She kissed him back feverishly. This night would be the beginning of many like it. Neither one knew how to tell Big Tina they wanted each other.

Burning It Down

While Mike and Tina's marriage was coming to an end, Mark was still trying to maintain his relationship with Gina. He couldn't help but notice there was differences in what his bank notes said and what was actually coming and going. He noticed there was shut off notices in the mail for utilities. This was something he was not used too. He confronted Gina about the notices he had found sitting on top of the garbage. Gina tried to claim she had absent mindedly forgotten to pay the bill. Mark then showed her the letter he received from the bank showing where the company had hot checks. Gina didn't have a clever story or excuse to make up in the moment.

"Fine Mark, you wanna know the truth? Well the truth is the business isn't doing good and I have been hoping you would see it and turn it around. I am tired of being the only one who notices how broke we are!" Gina made this declaration with venom in her voice. It was like she was daring Mark to argue with her.

"OK, so, you noticed the finances were in the toilet, but you didn't bother to tell me? I made you the damn book keeper, it is your JOB to tell me these things Gina!" Mark spat back at her.

The entire situation was absurd, of course, it was her job but what she was holding back was that she had been paying out some extra money on the side. She knew she looked like a fool in his eyes at the moment, but she couldn't tell him the truth. Gina had her own itinerary; she didn't plan on telling him anytime soon. Joe was her new play thing. She gave him extra pay to make sure he stayed in her pocket. Gina didn't know if that was really needed but she decided it was good insurance. She had also made a few other investments around Ardmore she had a plan to get the next thing that she wanted but she couldn't do it without the help of some of the town's higher ups. Gina had been a very busy girl. Not every night out had been to a bar, but that wasn't what was important now. Now she needed to get Mark off her ass.

Gina had grown bored, and when that happened it spelled trouble for anyone around her. The people who paid the price of her boredom were all too often the closest people to her. Since the fight that had sent her to Mike and Tina's for the night she had only grown colder, more calculating. She was going to use Mark, Joe, and anyone else she could to get what she wanted when she wanted.

There was a second bank account that Gina had opened and was funneling money into. The business wasn't bad, she was stealing off the top and hiding money away. Mark wasn't aware of her bank account, she had all of the bank statements sent to her mother's house. He was none the wiser and truly thought they were in a financial strangle hold. So, when Gina proposed an idea to get things on the right path again Mark listened.

"Baby, I know a way we can fix this and get back on top." Gina told Mark one night as they lay in bed.

"What?" Mark asked with little hope in his voice. He was watching all that he had built slowly sinking.

"Insurance, we have a lot of coverage on this house." Gina said, waiting for his response with bated breath.

"What are you getting at Gina? If we do anything to this house, we will go to jail" Mark responded sternly.

"Look, if we make it look like an accident, we can burn this house to the ground. Things are replaceable. We wouldn't use gasoline or anything that would prove arson. I know we can pull this off. Collect our insurance and things will get better." Gina was talking about it casually.

Mark didn't reply for a few minutes he was thinking about her proposal. They did risk getting caught but she did have a point. If they could do it without it appearing as arson, then they could cash in on the six figures. It was tempting he didn't want to lose his businesses. He had worked too hard for his accomplishments. He reached a decision.

"Ok, how do you think we should do it?" Mark asked her.

"I was thinking something small, something that would definitely be ruled an accident. I have been thinking about it, what if we leave my curling iron in the dirty clothes basket. Leave the house and we come back to our precious home in ashes." Gina said with ease.

Mark was shocked that she had it all planned out, but he couldn't deny that it sounded fool proof. He felt uneasy but his desire to keep what he had was stronger than his moral sense in that moment. He agreed to the plan, he didn't bother asking Gina why, or how she had decided on this. Mark wasn't sure he wanted to know how she came up with the idea. He decided to do it and that was all that mattered right now.

He had never committed a crime and Gina seemed a little too comfortable with it. He did fear that if he didn't go through with it that he would lose her and that wasn't an option for him. He loved her and would walk through hell if she asked. Mark had never loved another person so much in his life. He knew burning the house would be wrong, but it felt more wrong in his heart to lose her. Gina was his ride or die, and he felt he would die without her.

The next day they prepared, Gina removed the pictures of her and Mark together, leaving everything else. Nothing in the house mattered to her, she looked at everything as replaceable. Mark carried the hamper into the bathroom, Gina started the curling iron and left it under a couple of highly flammable pieces of clothing. They left the house and went to work. They acted like normal and no one suspected anything was off with either one of them. For

Gina the charade was easy, Mark did his best, his performance was good enough. Joe didn't know what was going on, Gina had left him out of the loop on this. They didn't need to run the risk of anyone knowing.

Within a few hours they received a phone call from the police station. Their house had burned, not completely but it wasn't able to be occupied. They raced to the house and Gina put on an amazing performance. Mark looked down trodden, he was letting guilt eat at him. Gina hogged the lime light, front and center complete with tears, and devastation on her face. They moved in with Mark's parents while the fire and insurance claim were sorted out. Mark and Gina didn't have the most comfortable stay but that was due to Gina insisting on disrespecting Mrs. Allen every chance she had. Gina always made sure they were alone when it happened then would cry to Mark about it.

"God, Mark, your mom is so mean to me! I can't do anything right. She says awful things to me! She said I am lazy and need to help more. I don't think it is my place to clean up after *your* family"

"Gina, for gods sakes, just do what she asks. We are in their house." Mark would respond.

Gina hated that she couldn't turn Mark against his parents, but he was close to them. Especially his dad. Dad had taught him everything he knew; it was Mr. Allen that had owned the first upholstery shop that supported his family. Mark wasn't going to disrespect them in their own house. If it weren't for them, he would be stuck at Gina's moms house living in true filth.

Mark's mom was putting up with her fair share of being disrespected, glared at, and cleaning the mess that Gina would leave in her wake. While she was cleaning one day, she poked her head in the couple's room to see it needed straightening up. As she was picking up dirty clothes off the floor, she noticed a box poking out from under the bed. It didn't have a lid on it nor was it taped shut. Mrs. Allen could see a family photo sitting atop some picture albums.

Mrs. Allen reached under the bed and pulled the box rest of the way out. To her surprise it was filled with family photos and a few other sentimental trinkets that she recognized as Mark's. Mrs. Allen reached in and pulled the albums out. It was family photos of Mark and Gina's families, plus photos of them together. All things that Gina had told every one had been engulfed in the house fire.

When Mark and Gina got home that evening Mr. and Mrs. Allen were waiting to question the couple. Asking why those items were there safe and sound? Hadn't Gina told her that the house fire had consumed all of their precious belongings? Gina tried to sputter out denials but Mark stopped her. He couldn't lie to his folks any longer. He admitted to them setting the fire. Mr. and Mrs. Allen were disappointed in the fact that Mark would have done this but they also knew he wouldn't have done it without Gina's extreme pressure. They were shocked to say the least but they kept their son's secret. With much disapproval and heavy hearts, they kept the secret to protect their child.

Even though Mark's parents kept his secret they told the couple to use the money to renovate the home and get moved back into it. They were not going to be a part of any scheme to help them get ahead by burning the house, so that is what Mark and Gina did.

Pain of Loss and Gain

A year had passed, Mark and Mike's dad passed away. This was devastating for the whole family, but the loss of Mr. Allen was particularly hard on Mark. Mark had idolized his dad, he spiraled into a deep depression. Mark couldn't accept the loss of his hero, his idol, his best friend, his dad. It became one the darkest periods in Mark's life. He felt an emptiness that he couldn't explain, and nothing could fill the void, Mrs. Allen had divided Mr. Allen's things between their children. Mike and Big Tina received Mrs. and Mr. Allen's bedroom suite. Mark and Gina received their items, as did James and Lisa. Gina didn't have any sympathy for what Mark was going through. Instead she used this time to see how far she could push her limits with him.

Gina took to going back out during the night without asking or bothering to tell Mark she would be leaving. There was a local dive bar that happened to be a popular watering hole for Ardmore's finest along with people that were considered to be less than favorable. It was on one of these outings that she met a man named Tim. Tim was a red-haired, pale, lanky, and unattractive man.

When Gina approached him, he wasn't sure if he was so drunk that he was imagining it or if she was so drunk, he was hitting the jack pot. Either way he welcomed her advances, and he felt like a cork about to burst from a bottle of shaken champagne. Tim was automatically in the 'Gina trap' but he didn't care if he was being used. Just to be close to a woman like her made him giddy.

Gina sat across the table from Tim, he had been sitting alone drinking a beer after he had already downed a few shots of tequila. Gina was still sober; she needed her wits about her in order to find another Joe Lane.

She felt like she needed another lacky to help ensure she could continue the activities she was currently engaged in. Tim seemed to fit the bill, she found him slightly stupid but not too stupid. He wasn't attractive, so she didn't think Mark would find him a threat, and to top it all off with a cherry he was morally flexible. Once she uncovered enough information about him, she began to drink. She wasn't going to be able to ignore him and expect to use him, but she needed liquor for the deed she was going to carry out in the parking lot.

Once she was drunk enough, they went out to his truck, there she used her body once again to ensure his future services. Much to her disgust he wanted more than she wanted to do but she let him do what he wanted to her. When Gina returned home in the wee hours of the morning, she took a scalding shower to get the feeling of Tim off of her.

Mark had passed out drunk and didn't even realize Gina had been out the previous night. Gina lucked out that he didn't notice, he hadn't been paying her the attention that she was accustomed to.

Mark dressed in his jeans and t-shirt and tried to wake Gina, but she was dead to the world, 'poor thing' Mark thought 'I must really be wearing her out.'

Mark had no idea that she was back to going out, not yet. Mark spent much of his time with his mom and Gina resented him to Hell and back for it, but he wasn't going to leave her during this hard and painful time. He decided to go visit his mom and siblings, James and Lisa. The home he had last shared with his dad there felt empty to him now, he was trying to climb out of the darkness, but he was never going to be able to fully accept his father's death. After a brief visit he began to feel antsy and took off.

Mark went into work, he needed to get his mind off everything. Joe was there working on a wrecked car that had come in a couple days prior this would be a good payday. Mark was so in tune to the work that he was able to assess the situation quickly.

"Joe, you need to have started at the rear bumper. Man, you should know this stuff, work your way forward. Why would you start with the door?" Mark corrected his employee.

"I, I um, I'm sorry Mark. I'll get down there and work on it. I'm sorry about your dad." Joe said.

Mark just looked at him, "thanks" that was all he could say. He then instructed Joe to start removing the bumper, and he would call in for a replacement. Mark walked into the office to make the call, sitting behind Gina's desk he thought to himself about how Joe could be such a screw up sometimes, but Gina always insisted they keep him on. She felt he was worth the training he lacked and that he could be valuable to the business. Mark never understood her thinking, but he couldn't afford to pay a licensed body guy for the time being. Mark got the bumper ordered and went back to the garage.

Mark helped Joe remove the bumper, then instructed him to start on the left and he would take the right, they needed to work down the car and strip it. Mark worked absent mindedly thinking about his dad and how he would never see him again. He tried to hide the pain on his face and after a couple hours the car was stripped. Mark stood back and assessed the damage, he couldn't believe the insurance company hadn't totaled it but who was he to say anything, it was work.

Gina came strolling in mid – day the previous night's exploit with Tim had left her hung over, but she had to hide it. She did a good job of hiding the bags under her eyes with makeup. She took her spot at her desk and started writing up the job that was sitting in the garage. Gina did her best to avoid Mark, she knew he would be able to tell something was going on with her. Joe on the other hand, she didn't bother trying to avoid him. He walked in the office and sat across from her on his lunch break. Mark was too pre- occupied with delving into work to notice. He had gotten used to Joe looking at Gina like a lost puppy, he didn't think she would ever cheat on him with such a loser.

"Gina, when can we see each other again?" Joe asked in a quiet voice.

God, she wished he would stop acting like this. It was driving her crazy.

"I don't know Joe, maybe when you become a success like Mark? I don't have time for this, I have too much going on." Gina replied coldly.

Gina never felt that she was neglectful to her and Mark's relationship, but she wasn't able to see herself in a negative light. The ability that most people have to look in a mirror and realize their wrongs and feel guilt for them was lost on her.

She didn't feel that way, she never felt the need to put herself in check she only felt the need to not get caught in her lies. Gina was a text book sociopath. She lacked the ability to feel guilt, remorse, sympathy, and she had no empathy. Gina had just begun her decent into the criminal underbelly of Ardmore. She always had a plan, and she was almost ready to start carrying it out, God help anyone who got in her way.

Chasity

There was a woman that Mark and Mike had known since they were young teenagers. She had always been a great friend to both brothers, Mark happened upon her one evening when he made a run to the convenience store for beer. Chasity was in line behind him, he hadn't noticed her, but she seen him and tapped his shoulder. Mark turned around and she was beaming at him. Mark couldn't help but return the smile, they hugged and once outside they talked for a bit.

Chasity told Mark she was sorry for his loss and congratulated him about Gina and his businesses. At this he lowered his head and mumbled a 'thank you.' Chasity noticed the change in his demeanor, she asked if he had a pen and paper. They walked to his truck and she used his scrap paper and a pen to jot her number down. She told him to call her if he needed anything. Mark thanked her and put the number in his wallet. He felt good seeing such a sweet friend, one that he hadn't seen in a long time.

Mark hoped that in time he would become accustomed to the way Gina had become, but through all the grief he still noticed she wasn't there for him through the death of his father. Gina wasn't the woman he had initially fallen in love with. Mark only knew that she was a real bitch these days. All she ever did was want for things, not him, not his touch. It broke his heart because she was all he wanted and all he felt he needed to be 'ok' in this life. Now after seeing Chasity he felt something welling up in him that he had not felt in a very long time. He felt attraction to another woman, he reached in his pocket and felt the piece of paper that held her phone number on it. He deliberated for the next couple of days before he made the phone call to Chasity.

As the phone rang, he felt nervous, what would he say? Then he heard a sweet voice pick up on the other end.

"Hello."

"Hey, is this Chasity?" Mark asked.

"Yeah, who's this?"

"It's Mark, I know you said call if I needed anything, but I was just wondering if you would want to hang out sometime?" Mark asked her.

"Yes! I would love to. When and where?" Chasity responded with an upbeat tempo.

"Um, how about the lake, say Saturday night?"

"Sounds great, I can't wait to see you! Call me between now and then to set up a time." Chasity said.

They hung up and Mark felt a mixture of elation and guilt. He tried to push these feelings aside, after all he hadn't done anything right? He argued with himself. Mark knew that Gina would be up to something Saturday night, she always was. He knew getting out to see Chasity wouldn't be difficult. He finally decided to put the guilt under a rug and forget it. He was going to hang out with an old friend and nothing more. He kept this information to himself, luckily Joe hadn't been around to overhear the conversation. Joe would have run to Gina like a lost puppy and barked the information to her in no time flat.

He was her superior lacky, and if he kept doing a good job then he would keep getting to be with her from time to time. Joe was good with their arrangement he didn't see any other women because he held on to hope that Gina would fall for him. He didn't realize how delusional his thoughts were. Gina wasn't looking for love, she had Mark. She was on the prowl for other things, material things, the freedom to lay with who she wanted without any consequence. All Joe Lane was to her was a puppet. One that she had to pat on the head and feed every once in a while, to keep him complacent.

Mark spent the week working and looking forward to seeing Chasity on Saturday. It was Friday now, and he watched Gina closely. She was oblivious that he was keeping an extra eye on her. He didn't want her to ruin his plans. He figured knowing his luck this would be the one Saturday that she decided to keep her ass at home. He noticed her talking on the phone with more animation in her movements than usual, he went in the office after she had hung up the phone.

"What was that all about?" Mark asked.

"Oh, nothing really, Miranda is having a bachelorette party tomorrow night. She was inviting me."

"Are you going?"

"As long as it's good with you Babe." Gina said, looking at him and grinning. That grin he loved so much.

"Yeah, you should go. She is your best friend I wouldn't stop you from that." Mark responded feeling a twinge of guilt yet feeling suspicious of her.

"Good! Thanks Babe. It starts at seven and I don't know when I will be home."

"Ok, well I hope you have fun. I think I will go see my mom." Mark said.

Mark called Chasity and set up a time to meet her at the lake. He told her to bring a swim suit and they would swim and have a few drinks. Chasity was beside herself she had missed Mark and Mike so much since they had both moved on with their lives.

It was Saturday at last, Gina and Mark both left work in good spirits. Gina rambled on about the party she was attending, and Mark listened as if it were truly interesting to him. When evening rolled around Gina took off dressed to the nines. Mark hurried and grabbed his swim shorts and an ice chest. He stopped by the store, filled up the ice chest with beer and some hard lemonade. Then pulled in Chasity's driveway. She was sitting on her porch in anticipation. She had on a bikini, with cut off shorts covering her bottom, and a beach towel. Her smile lit Mark up and he smiled too. It was the first real smile he had cracked in several months.

They arrived at the lake thirty minutes later. The place was fairly empty considering it was a hot summer night and a weekend. They discussed this fact for lack of anything better to discuss at the moment. Mark told Chasity to find a place she wanted to set up while he grabbed the ice chest and lawn chairs. She found a place right on the bank, with low hanging branches from the trees behind them.

Mark approached her with the ice chest in tow. Chasity slipped off the cut off shorts and walked to the water. Mark's heart did a little flutter, she was really pretty, and he had been lonely for so long. He sat down the chest and popped the top on a beer, he waded into the water where Chasity was going under to wet her hair. When she came up from the water, he handed her one of the hard lemonades.

They both drank and teased each other. It wasn't like when they were younger, this was elevated, it felt carnal and emotional. They were both feeling the change in the atmosphere. Chasity kept getting closer to Mark a little at a time until her drinks had made her heady enough to touch him. She tried to be innocent about it, but soon they were wrestling around in the water, hands touching bodies. Mark felt alive. Chasity felt the same. The sun was about to dip behind the horizon and they would have to exit the lake due to snakes.

They exited the refreshing water together, hand in hand. Once they had reached the bank Chasity decided it was now or never, she turned to Mark and pressed her body against his. Mark was more aware of his body than he had been in months, he didn't push her away or pull back. Slowly with some apprehension their faces came closer and soon they were mouth to mouth. This was the beginning of many more nights together.

I Don't Love You

After Mr. Allen passed away nothing would ever be the same. Mark lived in a dark and ugly place in his head, he missed his dad more than anything. He was encompassed in all consuming grief. Gina was out taking full advantage of his state of mind.

On the other side of town Mike was going through his own conundrum. He was ready to leave Big Tina but he knew it was going to be ugly. Telling someone you don't love them anymore never is a pretty sight. Little Tina had him convinced that now would be just a good a time as any. She was tired of waiting for him to leave her best friend. Mike knew the family wasn't going to take the news graciously, they all loved Big Tina, everyone but him.

Mike and Mark were sitting at a bar that Saturday night. Mike was trying to help coax Mark out of his depression. Little Tina was there too, not by invitation it was a coincidence. While the brothers sat at their table in the smoke - filled bar, Little Tina had snuck up behind Mike somewhere between the clacking of pool balls and the blaring juke box.

Sliding a hand on his chest while standing behind him, she nipped his ear playfully. Mike sat there like a statue Mark raised an eyebrow.

"Hey sexy, are you still with that fat ass?" Little Tina asked over the near deafening music.

"uh, yeah I am" Mike stated, trying to not look guilty.

Little Tina walked around to his side now, she grabbed his chin and kissed him sensually. She didn't care if Mark saw them, she knew she would be in the family soon.

"Well, if you ever leave that cow you know how to find me." She winked at the guys as she walked away.

Mark was more than curious but Mike acted completely aloof. Mark had his own secret and didn't judge his brother on his. The two men didn't discuss the complete awkwardness that had just happened. Soon they were far enough into their drinks that Mark had let the awkward encounter leave his mind. Mike knew he had to make a move sooner rather than later.

Sunday morning rolled around and Mike's head was pounding with a hangover. He reached for the ibuprofen and water Big Tina had left out for him on their night stand. 'She really is a good woman' Mike thought to himself. Regardless, he wasn't in love with her anymore and that fact wasn't going to change. When he finally climbed out of bed he headed for the kitchen in search of more hydration and coffee. Big Tina was in the living room watching a VHS tape of Barney for the one hundredth time with their son.

"Good morning babe." She said to Mike

"Mornin" he muttered back.

Big Tina followed him to their room, she could feel something was off with her husband.

"What's the matter Mike? You haven't been yourself."

"Nothing really, just got a hangover."

"No, it's more than that, tell me what's going on with you."

Mike sat on the bed next to his wife, digging around for the courage to just tell her. He let out a long sigh.

"Look, I don't know how to say this so I'm just going to say it… I want a divorce."

He had done it he had finally uttered the words to his wife. Big Tina sat there in shock and disbelief.

"What? Why?" Big Tina asked with tears brimming around her eyes.

"It isn't fair to you Tina I don't want to keep being here with you when I really don't feel the same anymore."

"Then get the HELL OUT!" She screamed at him through her tears.

Mike packed his belongings he told his son bye with a heavy heart and left the house. He drove straight to Little Tina's place. She answered the door quickly and bid him to come inside. It didn't take long for everyone to find out they had become an item. News like that travels at lightning speed. Mike felt a measure of guilt but not near enough to keep him with Big Tina. When she found out it nearly killed her.

Then after a few months after the divorce, news of Mike and Little Tina were expecting a child spread like wild fire. The couple was under a high amount of scrutiny after the speed of which they had gotten together and then announced they were having a baby. One thought that did plague Mike was that of how much his dad would have disapproved of how he had done this. Mr. Allen had loved Big Tina like his own daughter.

Mike knew how his father had felt about his now ex-wife, he decided the bedroom suite that had once belonged to his parents should stay in his family but he gave it to Mark. He knew in his heart that his dad would have flown off the handle if he had thought a whore like Little Tina would end up in it.

Material Things

Mark and Chasity had been having an affair for several months now, and he didn't feel guilty about it anymore. She listened to him and she made him feel like a man.

Gina was always wanting more and more material things it was 1995 and now she was wanting a new house. Mark agreed to the change. He loved Gina but he appreciated the way Chasity made him feel. Mark knew he didn't love Chasity, his heart belonged to Gina. Even with all of her crap he still loved her and wanted her happy. Gina decided they should build a house rather than buy one. She wanted something that she designed to her exact taste. Mark bought the land to build her new house on. It was a beautiful few acres and Gina was actually happy with the location.

Mark had become easier to deal with and Gina didn't fail to notice the change in him. She didn't question it, right now she was taking advantage of his passive demeanor. They were about to hit a snag in the building of their home, neither of them anticipated the reality of how long it would take to build with their cash. Mark refused to take out a loan on his businesses, and this left Gina to conspire how she would get the money. She certainly wasn't going to touch the money in her hidden account. Ardmore Oklahoma and Dallas Texas, approximately 100 miles apart, she devised a way to get the money.

Gina approached Mark while he was rebuilding a truck in the garage. She had what she felt was a fool proof plan, she had talked him into arson she thought she could talk him into her new money-making idea.

"Baby, I need to talk to you. It's important." Gina startled Mark as he had been in deep thought, he was always in the zone when he was working.

"What is it?" He said with concern.

"Well, I have been thinking of a way we could finish the house. No loans or owing out any money."

"I don't like the sound of this." Mark said squinting a bit as he looked at her.

"Just listen to me. Dallas is practically across the state line. What if I open a checking account in Texas? I can get the money we need before the checks ever hit the bank. I don't think they can prosecute over state lines." While Gina was making her proposal, Mark let out a deep sigh.

"Whatever Gina, you will do what you want anyway. Sounds like you have it all figured out. You better keep my name away from that shit though, I ain't risking jail time." Mark replied to her with a stern tone.

"No problem, I already asked Joe to help me. Me and him are both going to open checking accounts. We are gonna get what we need and be done with it. You and the business won't have any ties to it." Gina responded.

"OK Gina, sounds pretty fool proof... I guess. Why Joe?"

Gina rolled her eyes "for more money."

"OK"

That was Mark's response to her idea. Once again, he was going to let her have her way. He didn't particularly like the idea, but he wasn't going to argue. Mark learned long ago that arguing with Gina was completely pointless. Somehow, she would always get her way in the end. Gina was his weakness even when he tried to not let her be his Achilles heel. He was still seeing Chasity, but he could only picture Gina when they made love.

He wished that Gina would treat him the way Chasity did. He knew it wasn't fair to Chasity, but she also knew he had no intentions of leaving Gina for her. Chasity pretended she was fine with the arrangement but, deep down, she wanted Mark completely. Being his mistress was fun for a while, but she loved him now, she knew Mark didn't love her, but she went through the motions none the less.

Gina wasted zero time letting Joe know that Mark had said 'yes' about the Texas checking account scheme. Joe was just as jovial as she was, he hadn't ever got to spend this much time alone with Gina. Besides blindsiding the banks, he was letting his imagination go wild with possibilities of what he and Gina would do in Dallas. Joe was practically a slobbering mess just thinking of getting to touch her again. Gina on the other hand was taking this trip with purpose, appeasing Joe was the last thing on her mind.

However, there was something else she was thinking about. Gina knew that they would be gone for several days, and she wondered if Mark was up to anything. She didn't know what it might be, but she felt something *off,* until now she had ignored it, but she knew he had given in too easy about the checks. Gina called her new friend Tim from the bar and asked him to tap the phones while she was gone. Tim quickly agreed, he had worked as an electrician, something this small was no problem for him. He would just have to wait until Mark wasn't around.

Gina was pleased and felt comfortable to leave now. She would have eyes on Mark even when she wasn't around. It gave her the tingles to feel powerful. She and Joe made it to Dallas in no time, they rented a room and prepared to stay for a few days. Joe was exhilarated at having Gina all to himself, it was kind of pathetic really. He saved himself for her and watched Mark for her and now he thought he would get his chance to show her how he really felt about her. Joe had saved enough money to buy an engagement ring, the sap intended to pop the question after they were settled in and had dinner.

Back home Mark called Chasity and invited her to hang out at his and Gina's house while Gina was gone. Chasity eagerly agreed, she was going to get to play house for a few days. She hoped during this time he would view her in a different light, she had some news for him and couldn't wait to share it. Mark was ready to welcome her into the house for a few days and anticipated the pleasure of feeling her body next to his. If he could just stop loving Gina, Chasity would have been the perfect woman for him. He couldn't though, Mark wouldn't even entertain the thought. He belonged to Gina and she belonged to him. Affair or not the fact that Gina was his first priority would never change.

Back in Dallas Joe and Gina were heading back to the hotel after a wonderful and pricy meal at a local steakhouse. Gina hadn't begun to eat as much as Joe, but she was comfortable and getting sleepy. She was day dreaming about the hotel bed and getting comfy. Joe had other plans he touched the outside of his jeans pocket to feel the circular pattern of the ring he was so sure would make Gina love him. Once they were back in the room Gina went into the hotel bathroom to get a shower. Joe asked to join her, she informed him she was too tired to do anything. He wasn't fazed, he waited patiently for her to come out. When she walked back into the main room with the beds, he had sitting out a bottle of wine and two glasses. He asked Gina to take a seat at the little hotel table and he sat across from her. He poured them a glass each, as Gina was taking a drink, he got on one knee in front of her. Gina's eyes widened, she was confused but curious.

"Gina, I know that I could make you happy if you would give me the chance. I know how much we mean to each other. The nights we have spent together have been the best of my life. I would give you everything I own, including my heart, well, you already own that. Um, what I am trying to say is… will you marry me?" Joe held the ring up to her.

"Ha! Are you serious? I wouldn't marry you Joe. You are just my employee I don't feel that way about you. Why in the Hell would you think I could ever want to *marry* you?" Gina scoffed and belittled the man.

Joe stood up quickly, making long strides to the hotel door, he slammed it on his way out. He was so humiliated; he knew that she might say 'no' but dammit she didn't have to talk to him like he was dirt under her feet. That is how Gina viewed him though, like dirt under her feet. She would never marry the likes of him. In her mind he was just a pawn, a way to relieve boredom occasionally and someone to watch Mark for her. Joe decided to help with the check scheme all the same. He would do it, but now he was hurt and angry. He wasn't going to tell her how much she had hurt him.

Joe spent the evening and long into the night stewing on how he could hurt her back.

Joe wasn't the brightest crayon in the box, but he knew what would hurt her. He was going to wait for an opportunity to surprise her with it though, then maybe she would feel the way he felt now. He returned to the room when he figured she would be asleep. He laid next to her, watching her sleep and planning, his mind was now full of rage toward this woman.

Construction Destruction

Back in Ardmore Chasity was biting her nails while she sat on the sofa. Mark wouldn't be home for a couple more hours and she really wanted to talk to him. She could have called him she supposed but what she wanted to discuss needed to be face to face. She wanted him to be looking her in the face when she made her declaration. Chasity felt about Mark much the same as Joe felt about Gina. She knew she could give him a better life than Gina. Chasity knew that she would never hurt him and would always be there for him. It was hard for her to accept that he was unwilling to call things off with Gina, she didn't like being 'the other woman' and tonight she was going to tell him everything.

Gina and Joe had opened bank accounts at two different banks each in Dallas. With their new check books in hand they went on hefty shopping sprees. Joe had driven the company truck to load as much as they could, they were 'buying' building material for Gina's house. Joe, to Gina's surprise, was well aware of the items they would need. He would give her a list and he would take the other portion of supplies needed, they would separate in the store and make the purchases using their fraudulent accounts. To the two of them it felt like winning free money, so they spent to their hearts content. Gina was going to have everything she wanted in this home.

The pair rented a U-Haul truck to fill up with the supplies. Gina didn't want to have to keep traveling to Dallas. She also kept in mind the faster they could get it done the faster they could get back to Oklahoma before law enforcement would catch on to them.

Gina tended to think ahead and that was one thing that helped her in life. She always managed to stay a step or two ahead of the destruction she was about leave in her wake. She would already have a way of making herself look innocent and the victim. Gina was a pure deviant and people were still blind to how far her deception could and would go. Her kind wasn't anything that the people in her immediate life was used to, looking back, no one is prepared for the desolation a psychopath can leave in their wake.

Mark came walking in the house to find supper waiting on him. That was a nice change he thought to himself. Of course, Gina never had dinner waiting on him, but he didn't expect it from her. He had grown accustomed to fending for himself at dinner time. Mark wasn't going to be petty and gripe her out for not cooking, she worked at the shop too, even if it had become more part time now days.

He showered and thanked Chasity for the home cooked meal. It was absolutely delicious, pork chops, mashed potatoes, green beans and corn on the cob. Damn it was good; he was busy stuffing his face and didn't notice the way Chasity was watching him devour her cooking with a whimsical smile on her face.

Chasity dreaded the talk she needed to have with him, right now everything felt perfect even if it was just for a few days. She knew she had to rip the band aid off though. After dinner she got him a beer and they settled on the couch, she nuzzled up next to him. She sat looking at the television but not watching the program. She was working up the courage to talk to him about everything on her mind. Finally, after an hour had passed, she felt it was now or never.

"Hey, I need to talk to you about some stuff." Chasity said with a slight quiver in her voice.

"Yeah what is it?"

"First, let me ask you a question. Is there any chance that we could ever be a real couple?"

Mark looked down at the top of her head resting on his shoulder. He didn't want to answer this question because he already knew the answer and he knew it would break her heart.

"Look, I really like you a lot but…" Chasity stopped him mid – sentence.

"But you love Gina and you only like me." She said with a silent tear rolling down her cheek.

"I do love Gina, we have been through a lot together and I know she is difficult, but we have been together a long time. I don't think I could leave her." Mark felt a twinge of pain pulling at his heart as he heard the words come out of his mouth.

"Then why in the hell are you with me?" Chasity said in a snappy voice.

"Because I do like you and you make me happy in other ways that Gina can't. I don't think she means to hurt me, she's just *Gina*. I have been with her since I was nineteen." Mark really didn't have a better answer without completely destroying Chasity. What he didn't realize was that he already was destroying her.

"OK, well, I still need to tell you something. I'm pregnant." Chasity said rising to her feet and blocking the television.

Mark stayed seated he felt a rush of terror course through his body. This wasn't supposed to happen he could feel the fear from her words radiating through him. All he could think about is 'what if Gina finds out?'

"You better not be screwing with me Chasity." Mark said sternly.

"I'm NOT, here, LOOK." She reached in her back pocket and flung the positive pregnancy test at him.

Mark plucked it from his chest where it had landed and looked at the stick. It was positive, no doubt.

"Is there anyone else you have slept with?"

Chasity couldn't believe what she was hearing. "NO, just you!" She responded in a raised and hurt voice.

"What are we going to do? You won't be with me, but we have a child coming into this world and all you care about is Gina. I need answers Mark."

"You better keep your mouth shut about this; I mean it. I think you need to leave." Mark said coldly.

Chasity was devastated at what she was hearing coming from this man she thought she knew so well. The man she had allowed herself to fall for. She was shaking violently with anger she went upstairs and gathered her stuff. When she came back down, he was still sitting on the couch, but he had his head in his hands.

"Chas, I'm sorry. I really am but I can't be a part of this."

"Don't worry you don't have to be. I don't need you or anything you have. I did want you but now, I can't get far enough away from you." Chasity said crying so hard she could barely get the words out.

With that Chasity left, Mark listened as she pulled away and wondered if he had made the right choice. Of course, he had he told himself. God, Gina, what if Gina found out? He knew his thoughts were selfish, but he couldn't stop thinking about Gina now, he didn't want to live without her. He couldn't live without her, and he knew that if she ever found out about this she would be gone forever. Mark went to bed that night feeling a thousand pounds heavier. He didn't know what to do but he knew this had to remain between him and Chasity.

In Dallas Joe and Gina were in bed together after a thorough night of love making. She told Joe she was sorry for the way she had responded to his proposal and explained why she felt the way she did. Joe pretended it was all water under the bridge. He felt proud of himself, he had the upper hand he thought, and he would use it when the time was right.

Joe had no real intentions of forgiving Gina for practically laughing in his face when he laid his heart on his sleeve before her. She had ruined him, and he wanted to ruin her. Joe wanted to hurt her, disgrace and embarrass the almighty Gina. Until then he would keep enjoying the company she provided. He did his best to view her as just another piece of ass. Gina suspected as much but she wasn't worried at the moment, she too enjoyed the unspoken game they were playing.

Return

Several days had passed since Chasity had revealed her pregnancy to Mark. He still hadn't come to terms with it, so he decided to end any communication with her for now. Gina and Joe were on their way back from Texas after racking up a staggering fifty grand in hot checks. When Mark seen them pulling in with the truck and a giant U-Haul, he knew it had to be a hefty amount they had spent. He dismissed the thought of the money when he seen Gina's smiling face, and she was waving at him as she pulled the truck onto their land. She jumped out after parking and showered him with kisses and hugs. In spite of it all she really had missed him, and the guilt of Chasity swept over him like a wave at high tide.

"Wow, you guys really did get everything!" Mark was excited, even though he knew it was technically stolen materials. He was just feeling happy that work on the house could continue and Gina would be pleased with him.

"Yeah, it took a while to gather it all, but we have everything that had to be postponed. God, I am so excited Baby!" Gina said to Mark with elation.

"Joe, was she a handful?" Mark said laughing.

"More than you can imagine. Have you ever gone on a shopping spree with this woman?" Joe asked keeping his attitude in check, even adding a laugh.

"More than I can count. I'm glad you guys made it back safe and sound. Now we can get busy finishing this house." Mark replied.

"OK you two, I'm not that bad." Gina said playfully.

It was a good day Mark had his Gina home in one piece and Joe had been there to take care of her. He felt grateful to Joe for looking out for Gina. Mark hadn't heard from Chasity and he felt guiltier for being happy about it. He didn't want anything coming in between him and Gina.

The trio unloaded materials that day and Joe took the U-Haul back to a drop off point. When they finished their work late in the evening Joe dismissed himself and headed back to his shabby apartment. Gina and Mark headed back to their house and welcomed each other properly. After that they slept, for the first time in a while they both slept peacefully. Mark felt a burden had been lifted by breaking it off with Chasity and Gina, well, because for once she was actually too tired to lay awake and scheme. Her idea had gone off without a hitch and she felt good about it.

The weekend was soon over, and they returned to work like normal. Gina had been so busy making plans for her new house that she had absent mindedly forgot to check in with Tim regarding the phone tap. It wasn't until Tim came into the office at the lot to talk to her about it that she remembered.

"What are you doing here?" Gina hissed at him as he sat across the desk.

"Well there are two things, one, I need a job. Two, did you forget about the wiretap on your phones?" Tim said in a collected voice. For someone so homely he had the arrogance of an exotic flashy bird.

"Oh, yeah, what about the tap?" Gina asked looking over his shoulder to make sure Mark wasn't approaching.

"Well, here's the deal. Give me a job and I will give you the recording. I promise it will be worth your while." Tim said with a cocky air.

"Look, I have to talk to Mark before I can hire anyone. I want that recording." Gina was frustrated. She didn't appreciate being black mailed by a loser like him.

"Go ask him, I'll wait." Tim replied.

Gina rolled her chair back, she stood and walked to the garage where Mark was working.

"Babe, I have a fella who needs a job. He was an electrician I think he could benefit you and save time on some of these cars.

What do you think about trying him out?" Gina said with a fake wide smile. The kind of smile that doesn't reach the eyes.

"Well, we have Joe and the guys at the other shop, can we afford to hire anyone?" Mark asked her.

"I was thinking, Trevor, at the other location, he isn't top notch. I feel like he has had more than enough chances and this guy seems to really know his stuff. I was thinking we should just fire Trevor and let this guy take his place. He could float between here and there." Gina responded without batting an eyelid.

"OK sounds good babe, I will come in and meet him in a few minutes."

Gina went back into the office with a smug look as she glared at Tim.

"He is coming in to meet you." She said.

They sat in silence in the office waiting for Mark. When Mark came in a few minutes later he pulled Tim into the garage, he drilled him with questions regarding vehicle repair, electrical and wiring, asked him if he had a problem with floating between locations. Tim managed to impress Mark and landed a job. Mark told him to go see Gina and get a schedule and fill out his tax papers.

"Well, that was easy enough… here." Tim handed the small cassette to Gina.

Tim left, and Gina held the cassette in her hand, her curiosity was piqued through the roof. She went on a lunch break heading to the nearest radio shack and bought a tape player for this size tape. As she listened to the recordings her head felt like it was going to explode. *Chasity…* Gina had to find a way to confront Mark without him knowing he had been recorded. Gina felt no guilt about her trysts with men but now *she* felt completely betrayed. She decided she didn't care if he knew about the recordings, she was so furious she couldn't devise a plan to sneak it on him. She drove back to work and gave him the cold shoulder the rest of the day. Gina knew she was going to make him pay dearly when they got home.

Mark was confused at the sudden change in Gina's temperament, but he was used to it at the same time. He asked her what was wrong, but she gave him a flippant answer about arguing with her mom. Mark knew that wasn't anything new. He carried on with work under the assumption she was mad at her mom and let her be. The clock was ticking away to the verbal thrashing he was going to receive, and he was clueless to it.

"What the fuck Mark?!" Gina flung the recorder at him. Mark barely caught it before it hit the carpet.

He eyed the recorder curiously, then looked at Gina as he hit 'play' within a few seconds his stomach was on the floor. "Gina… I" She didn't let him finish.

"You have accused me of affairs, but I have NEVER cheated on you!" Gina let the tears stream down her face as her lies turned into truths as they hit Mark's ears.

Mark stood there dumbfounded, "Baby, she means nothing! I love YOU!" It was the best he had in the moment.

"How could you? How could you betray me like this? I love you I work my ass off for you and this is the thanks I get?" Gina kept spewing, playing the victim to perfection.

"I already broke it off with her babe! Please, can we talk about this calmly? Please Gina, I love YOU. I told her to kick rocks!" Mark was pleading.

Gina ran down the hall and locked him out of their bedroom. He felt like such a piece of crap for what he had done. Mark went to his mom's house and stayed a few days until Gina was ready to talk.

"I am ready for you to come home." Gina's voice on the other end of the line said.

"Are you sure?" Mark asked.

"Yes, I'm sure Mark. We have a lot to talk about and I want to work on this." She said flatly.

Mark didn't waste any time going back home to her. Her conditions were simple, zero contact with Chasity. He had already done that, her next condition was that he marry her.

"No, I told you when we met that I didn't want to marry anyone. I love you and I will do anything else, but I just can't marry you." Mark said.

His words were contradictory to the way he loved her, but he had made his mind up years previous that he never wanted to get married. Gina persisted on the subject and he denied her on this, this one thing he would not give into. It made his life hell in the months that followed but he stood firm.

Then as an act to try to force his hand Gina stopped her birth control. When she announced her pregnancy to him, he was over the moon. Gina felt that this was the way she would ensnare him into marriage. A way to manipulate him into being her legal husband. It didn't work, she whined, and when whining didn't work, she would have flat out explosive tantrums. Yelling and screaming at him, reminding him of what a sorry man he was. She tried to tell him it was his obligation to marry her.

Mark let her complaints and pouting fall on deaf ears. He knew he needn't marry her to be a father to their son and so far, she had not done a thing to change his mind on marriage. That was one of his 'foot down, no budging' stubborn traits. Mark never had the desire to marry, he loved her more than anything no doubt, but she would never get him down that isle.

Hello and Goodbye

There were babies being added to the Allen family left and right. Mike and Little Tina had a new baby girl, she was a beauty. Little Tina hadn't wanted to stay in Ardmore any longer though. The dirty looks and glares of suspicion that were cast her way were finally getting to her. The town as a collective felt she had killed her previous husband. His death had happened under too mysterious of circumstances. It was so highly improbable that anyone other than her had cut his brake lines. Ardmore residents would never buy into it being a freak accident or teenagers being malicious. Little Tina had inherited far too much insurance money for it to look like anything other than premeditated murder.

Mike gladly took her and their daughter and moved them to Dallas. He didn't want his wife and new baby to have to deal with the scrutiny that followed Little Tina everywhere she went in that town. Dallas was a reasonable distance from the burning gazes of the town's folks and he wouldn't have to worry about his daughter growing up with something so vile hanging over her head.

Meanwhile, Mark was dealing with his own personal battle. His son had been born, he didn't rush to the hospital to be with him and Gina immediately. Mark felt a heaviness in his heart, he wasn't ready for all of the 'congratulations' he was going to receive for his first child. No, he already had a child another son with Chasity. Of course, no one knew about this son and Chasity hadn't told anyone that Mark was the baby's father. Before He made the trip to Gina and his new born he went to Chasity's home. He didn't know why he felt the need to see her and his son. He had tried so hard to forget that it ever happened but his heart couldn't forget.

Mark was standing in the doorway when Chasity opened the front door, she felt a pang of hurt in her heart but she didn't turn him away. Mark came in and held his son, the son that he couldn't be a father to. He felt so much guilt and shame for not being there for this child, his own flesh and blood. He knew that he didn't have any other options. He cared about Chasity but he wasn't in love with her, Gina had won that place in his heart years ago. He sat down and coddled his child, taking in the boy's scent. Committing the baby's face and features to his memory. He hoped that one day, he could be the man that his son here needed but he knew today was not that day.

After Mark spent some time seeing his son, he bid Chasity a farewell and another apology. He didn't know if it really mattered to her or not. It prepared him to face his new son technically his second baby but his first to everyone else. Mark knew the truth and he knew it was time to play the role of first - time dad. And in ways it was his first time since he hadn't been a part of his and Chasity's son's life. He pulled out of the drive and made his way to the hospital to meet his new little one.

As Mark drove, he prepared himself mentally for all of the congrats that were going to be given, not really knowing if he deserved them or not. But either way he would accept the kind words. He arrived at the hospital, sitting in his truck he steeled himself for the barrage.

When Mark entered the room, he went immediately to Gina who was holding their little son. All of Mark's anxiety melted away as he kissed her forehead and reached down to hold his son. As he cradled the baby to his chest his eyes were gleaming with happiness. He felt the pride that only a new loving father can feel. He would never have to be parted from this baby, he would get to raise this child and be a real daddy to him. This was one moment that he knew could never be tainted or taken away from him. This was his new beginning.

"Hello, little one I am your daddy." He said beaming down at his amazing miracle. Mark was consumed with love in that room for his son and for Gina. He knew his life was going to be better from now on because he had something, someone to make it better for.

Texas Shopping Spree Comes Home

It took a good long year, but the hot checks finally came home to roost. Gina was shocked, she really didn't think they would come across state lines to look for her. She hadn't accounted for the sheer amount of money she had technically stolen either. It was a sticky mess and Mark was the only one who could bail her out of trouble. Gina was facing a lengthy stay in prison and Mark wasn't about to let that happen. She was the mother of his child, which made her more wonderful in his eyes.

They discussed their options and Mark hired an attorney, he was the best in Ardmore. Leo Whitman would be taking the case he was well respected and was also licensed to work in Texas. Joe hadn't been caught yet, so he didn't have anything to worry about. He figured if he got caught too that Mark would bail him out since he had done it for them to begin with. Leo quickly made a deal with the state that if she payed what she had taken in X amount of time that she wouldn't see prison. All they could do was put the house Mark had built up for sale.

Gina started acting 'off' after the near prison stay. She had managed to pretend to be normal for a little while but now she was ebbing her way back into being her normal self. The bigger their son grew, and her reprieve from jail caused her to regain her old appetites. This didn't go unnoticed by Mark. At first, he let it ride but she started her night time vanishing. He did not want to go down this road again. He didn't want to deal with the suspicions of her possibly having affairs, and he didn't want to deal with her not being a good parent. He decided to take a page out of her book, he tapped the phones. Only he didn't need help, he did it himself. Mark ultimately decided to invade her privacy because of her changing attitude and the constant phone calls.

Mark realized that if she answered the phone there wasn't any issues with prank calls but when he answered, it had become a habit for the caller to breath on the other end then hang up. It was happening frequently, and it was driving him to be suspicious. Mark wrestled with wanting to know and not wanting to know. He didn't know how he would react if she was cheating. In the end he made the decision to do the phone taps, and he waited.

Mark decided to let two weeks go by, he was a patient man. If she was doing anything that would be more than enough time to catch her. Two weeks was long enough to find out who, where, why and any other questions he had. In the meantime, he maintained a sense of normality for their son. He didn't let on like anything was different, and he didn't argue with her when she would leave at night and return at dawn. Mark was going to catch her and confront her with evidence, he hoped against hope there would be no evidence and that maybe she just had a drinking problem or something.

Gina was none the wiser, she had no idea he was tapping the phones at the business and at home. She went about her life as normal and like Mark, she tried to act like they had some normalcy. Gina didn't do this for their son, she did it to keep Mark off her ass. She didn't want him meddling in her life outside of their home, the one he had built with his own two hands. Gina didn't think in terms like that, she didn't appreciate the blood, sweat and tears that went into making the house. The one they now had to sell to pay her restitution for the hot check fiasco. It had been all for nothing in the end.

Mark drove to Dallas to see Mike and confide in him what he was doing, and the worries he had. Mike was happy to see his brother now; it had been awhile. Mike told Mark that he had seen Gina when she was there on business. Mark hadn't told Mike that it was illegal business. Likewise, Gina hadn't told Mark she had gone to see Mike and Little Tina. Mark just told Mike about the phone taps, and that Gina was being weird again. Mike didn't seem concerned about it. He just assured his brother that it would all be OK. After the brothers had spent the day talking and catching up Mark left not feeling any better about the entire situation.

Gina had never mentioned going to see Mike and Little Tina. Mark supposed she didn't have to, but it would've been nice to know. That bit of information was odd to withhold he thought to himself.

He paced around the empty kitchen, their son was sleeping, and she was gone again. The two weeks had wrapped up. Mark needed to check the phone taps. He called his mom to come watch Junior, she came over and sat at the house with her sleeping grandchild while Mark went to the shop to get the recordings. When he got back, he visited with his mom some and bid her goodnight, he was chomping at the bit to listen to these tapes.

Week One: Monday – Gina and what seemed to be a detective. Discussing a meeting for that night at the Ardmore Hotel.

Tuesday- Nothing suspicious

Wednesday- Derek? Marks friend that was also in the car business

Thursday- Gina and Leo Whitman making plans to meet at his office after hours.

Friday- Gina and the Detective- same arrangement

Saturday- Gina and an unknown male deciding to meet at the Ardmore Lake.

Sunday- Leo Whitman again

 Mark felt bile rising in his throat, she wasn't having an affair she was having a multitude of them. Gina was fucking the entire town. Mark felt himself slipping as he began to listen to the next set of tapes.

Monday- Gina and the unknown male again, lake arrangements

Tuesday- Gina and Officer **** Ardmore Hotel

Wednesday- Nothing

Thursday- Nothing

Friday- Leo Whitman

Saturday- The Detective

Sunday- Officer**** Ardmore Hotel

    Mark was sick, he was furious, he felt wrath that must have had Hell itself wrapped up inside the anger. In this moment he hated her, he was disgusted by her. He had been so stupid, he thought she might be doing something but dear god, she was the whore of the town and he was the laughing stock. It was now Monday and he didn't wait to listen to who she was with tonight. Mark found a bottle of bourbon and drank it all. He was waiting for her on the front porch when she finally came strolling in.

    When she seen him and the condition he was in, her smile quickly faded. 'What the hell?' She thought to herself. By sheer instinct she didn't climb the steps to the porch, he came down to meet her instead. Mark reeked of a brewery, he grabbed her by the arm and led her in the house. Gina stumbled up the stairs in her heels, asking him what in the world was going on? Mark slammed her onto the couch, now she looked at his face for the first time. His face was contorted in anger, in an alcohol fueled rage, she had never seen him like this. For the first time Gina felt scared of Mark. Mark didn't wait to answer her questions, he had the little cassette player, he pushed play and sat it on the coffee table.

In horror she listened to her phone calls, she tried to maintain her composure, but Mark lumbered behind her while she listened. After a few minutes she decided to try her 'tough girl' act.

"What the hell? Why are you spying on me? You had an affair first!" Gina yelled.

"No, no... NO MORE LYING! I know you have been fucking half the town, affairs like this don't just start out of nowhere! Leo? Are you kidding? That old fuck? Sick Gina, how... how do you even let a man like that touch you? My God... do you have any standards?" Mark was pissed and letting it all out. Her feelings were the last thing on his mind. He was not going to hold back.

Gina had begun to sob by this point, she had never seen Mark enraged. The tape kept playing in the background only adding fuel to the situation. Gina realized this and grabbed the cassette player and turned it off. Now, they were thrown into silence for a few moments. Mark reached behind his back and withdrew a nine – millimeter pistol from his waist band. He pointed it squarely at Gina.

Gina was frozen in place; all they had separating them was the couch. She slowly began to walk around the piece of furniture, trying to sooth Mark with apologies and reminding him of their son in the other room. When she was standing close enough, she put her hand on Mark's arm, he jerked away quickly and brought the butt of the gun down across the bridge of her nose, with a sickening crack; blood gushed out from her broken nose and she screamed out.

Mark couldn't believe that he had struck her, but he was fueled by intense rage and alcohol. He pulled out his cell phone and called his mom. Mark told her what he had done and what was happening, he told her he was going to kill himself, that he couldn't live like this. Mrs. Allen worked on talking him down while she sped to their house. When she walked in, she could see the situation was volatile, more than she had expected. Mark was sitting on the steps in the house, Gina sitting on the step below him with a broken nose, still bleeding and Mark had the gun to Gina's head. Mrs. Allen did all she could to try and diffuse the situation.

While she talked Mark stood up, "I'm leaving, Gina you can go screw yourself, or Ardmore, whichever." With that he left the house, Mrs. Allen and Gina could hear his truck going down the road. Mrs. Allen stood looking at Gina's face. She took care of the injury the best she could and checked on her grandson. Mrs. Allen's heart hurt for her grandchild.

She didn't like that he was living in a home that had become unstable. Mrs. Allen knew it had been coming but she knew Mark wouldn't have listened to her. Gina's deceit wasn't lost on her but even she hadn't known how far it ran until now. It was with a heavy heart Mrs. Allen left the house; Gina was reassuring her there was no need for her to be there. Her hands were tied, she would reach out to Mark tomorrow after he had slept off the whiskey and was settled down.

A Set Up

Mark was gone nearly a week. He wasn't answering anyone's calls, he was severely depressed and couldn't stand the thought of human interaction. He did give his guys at the shops instructions before disappearing. Mark didn't do any soul searching, rather he seethed on what Gina had been doing and who all she had been doing it with. Gina had been trying to get in touch with him, she wanted to fix things with him, she didn't want to be alone, primarily she didn't want to lose out on any money – making endeavors. She was incredible at getting Mark to see things her way, and she wasn't done yet.

Gina was relieved that there hadn't been any calls with Joe or Tim, that would have proved to be more disastrous than the current situation. She decided she would go see him at the hotel, she hoped he was there. He hadn't been to his mom's so unless he skipped town that's where he would be. Luck was on her side, Gina could see his truck parked at the Ardmore Hotel, she got his room number and made her way up to him. Knocking on the door she could hear the television playing, she waited then knocked again. This time she could hear shuffling around and a groggy "who is it?" from the other side.

"Babe, it's me please answer the door. We miss you so much at home. I want to work on this." Gina pleaded through the door, using the word 'we' so it would cause Mark to think of their son.

He opened the door and stood aside so she could walk in the room. Looking at her face guilt wrapped itself around him like a blanket. The room was dark, and rather dreary. Gina could see he had been doing a lot of drinking. She didn't care, she had come to him with an idea in mind. She needed Mark to help her carry out yet another dirty deed. Of course, she didn't start with that as her opening topic, first she had to convince him to come home.

"What do you want?"

"I know I can't take back what I have done. But I am hoping you could forgive me? We need to talk about this, and your son misses you like crazy. He asks where his daddy is every day." Gina was hitting all of Mark's soft spots.

"Dammit Gina, I don't know if I can. You have done some really bad shit to me. I want to see my son too, I miss the little guy like hell but me and you, I don't know if I can do it." Mark was being more honest with himself now than he ever had been since meeting Gina.

"You did it too you know? I am not the only guilty person, I may have done more, but you made me feel useless, and you never paid attention to me! You are always busy working, and I work too then we just never take time for one another." Gina was trying to make a good argument.

Mark was still feeling the effects of his week – long binge, in the end he gave up and went home with her. They were going to try again; he couldn't refuse her. Mark was literally blinded by love and he so easily fell into her traps. Sometimes he knew he was letting her manipulate him and sometimes he didn't but now, he didn't care anymore he just wanted to return home and fix things. In his mind they had indeed screwed each other over and now he wanted to put it behind them.

Gina had other plans, she always did, it never occurred to her that 'enough is enough.' To her the world was a great big grab bag and her greedy hands were always inside the bag. She would steal other people's turns if it meant she might come out with a grand prize from the grab bag. She was a lost person, she was so far gone by this point there was nothing going to stop her from getting what she wanted, what she felt like she was owed. There was no rhyme or reason to her thinking, sociopaths don't work logically, she only enjoyed the feeling of euphoria and God help the people who stood in the way of her and whatever shiny object she had her eye on at any given time.

Gina knew she was going to get what she wanted, she wanted it bad and she knew Mark well enough to know he would help her. First, she had a few loose ends to tie up though. Mark was about to see how far Gina would go for what she craved, but he wasn't ready for what she was going to ask of him. The house had sold the week Mark had spent drinking his sorrows away, she already had a new place picked out for them. It was such a beautiful home. Too bad they wouldn't be living there long.

A month went by and they were moved into the new house within Ardmore city limits. Mark was feeling a little crushed over having to sell the house he had built but he understood it was that or Gina was going to be sitting in prison. When he had to think in those terms it was a no brainer. Of course, he wasn't going to let her see jail. Then he thought bitterly to himself *'neither would one of those detectives she was banging.'* He had to dismiss the thought to keep his anger in check. Mark wasn't over the things she had done, no more than *she* was over Chasity. He often wondered how Chasity was doing and how the kid was, and he prayed Gina would never find out about the baby. While Mark was lost in thought on the subject of Chasity and the kid Gina walked into the kitchen where he was sitting.

"Mark, I think we should do it again."

"Do *what* again?" He asked her this, but he knew what she meant. The shops weren't doing terrible, but he knew they needed a financial reprieve.

"Look, you know we need the money, I won't involve you. I will have Joe help me. We can evict the tenants in our rent house and move back there. I don't need anything huge anymore. I'll have Joe help with this place, make it look lived in, but we need to move our stuff out without anyone noticing."

"Well, it's hard to argue when you have it so well planned. Fuck it, do it. I don't care." That was all Mark had to say on the matter. He knew he would be fighting a losing battle if he argued.

Gina enlisted Joe the next day, he was excited, he felt this could be his chance to finally get her back for the way she had emasculated him. Joe did everything that was asked of him, he helped move their most precious belongings with the cover of night. Then he helped fill the house with items that Gina purchased from the salvation army, giving the house the appearance that it was lived in.

The week before they had evicted the family that had been renting the first house they had owned in Ardmore. Gina decided to have Tim cause the actual fire, she trusted him more than Joe, she found Joe to be rather stupid and Tim had been an electrician. So, between the two men she enlisted Tim to do the 'heavy lifting.'

Mark and Gina took their son out the day the house was set to be caught on fire. Despite Gina not wanting Joe involved Tim didn't listen to her. He knew that Joe was already in deep between the hot checks and spying on Mark. Now, he knew that he needed a fall boy in case anyone seen anything. Tim wasn't the idiot that Joe was, he gave Joe instructions to enter the house and turn the gas on. Tim stayed outside, he had already pre planned and had a riding lawn mower rigged to set the house ablaze. Joe walked out of the house, got in his car and drove away. Tim watched Joe leave and crept from the side of the house where he had been hiding behind the air unit. Tim went to the lawn mower and started the ignition.

Tim slipped away like a snake in high grass, leaving the lawn mower to do its job. He hadn't needed any special electrician skills; he had simply stuffed the mower engine full of dead grass and leaves. It took a few minutes and the mower was shooting flames beneath the hood, sitting close enough to the house that was leaking gas. Within a few minutes the house caught fire. The incident made headlines. It was on the news and on the front page of the paper. Once again insurance paid the bill

Four Exits To Hell/ Allen

LONE GROVE

Riding lawn mower sparks house fire Sunday

By Wilbert Wiggs
Staff Writer

LONE GROVE — Backfire from a riding mower was listed as the cause of a fire resulting in extensive damage to a northside home Sunday afternoon.

Firemen were called out shortly after 4 p.m. by Marvin Mashburn, a neighbor who spotted flames shooting up the back of the home, 2.5 miles north of U.S. Highway 70 on Loftis Street, just off Meridian Lane. Eight units and nine firefighters responded.

Fire Chief Billy Christian said first reports traced the fire source to a riding mower parked near the northeast corner of the home, owned by either Sonja Daniels or Mark Allen. Firemen were advised the fire was spotted and reported by Mashburn, a neighbor to the south.

The first alarm came at 4:05 p.m. Firemen and equipment began leaving the scene at 4:50 p.m.

Flames scaled the wall to the roof and through a rear window into the kitchen of the small home. Fire damage was limited to that area of the home with firemen quickly controlling the burn. Smoke and heat damage was reported throughout the one-bedroom house.

Based on the initial investigation and available reports, damage was estimated at $25,000. The family had another home available for emergency housing.

Staff Photo/Wilbert Wiggs
This riding lawn mower was listed as the cause of a fire Sunday in Lone Grove.

Tim was pleased with his handy work when a neighbor reported seeing Joe entering and exiting the property minutes before the fire. Joe officially had a warrant out for his arrest and it wasn't long before he was picked up by the ADP. Joe was questioned about the reason he had for being in the home that day. Joe told police that Mark had asked him to pick up some parts needed at the shop. Mark corroborated the story… for now.

The Fall

Gina and Mark had been running a side business. It was one that would have landed both of them in prison. The car lot had been being used as a chop shop. Joe had been privy to this, he helped run the scheme. It was a simple way to make big bucks and both Gina and Mark had become addicted to the extra income their racquet produced. They had an iron clad way of doing things.

The chop shop was something Mark and Gina had been running with Joe for a long time now, the operation was simple. Joe would test drive a car from a car lot and while he was out, he would pass the key off. Tim would make a copy of the key and later that night Joe and Tim would go to the car lot they had used and steal the car from the lot. After altering the Vin numbers, they would slap a new coat of paint on the car. Simple enough, then the vehicle would go up for sale or be ran through an auction.

After the fallout Mark and Gina had with her affairs, she had convinced Mark that the affairs had been in their best interest. Mark hadn't understood at first. However, Gina had made things clear to Mark and it had appealed to the side of him that wanted big money as well.

It had begun after their reconciliation, a few days after Mark had come back home to Gina. Gina had approached Mark regarding Leo Whitman in particular, she explained since he was Mark's attorney and not hers that they could blackmail him into anything. Anything was one hundred thousand dollars. Gina and Mark had kept this between themselves, but Gina had convinced Mark to let her set up a meeting with the attorney. She said she would get him on tape divulging private information regarding Mark and get his admittance of their affair on the tape. Mark agreed to this, they sat up the meeting and Gina did as she said she would. Mark had waited in the parking lot waiting for Gina to come back with the needed tape.

Gina did not disappoint; Mark went into the attorney's office and played the tape back to him. Mark then made the demand for the money or the recording was going to go public and Leo Whitman's good standing would be ruined, and he would lose his wife not to mention his right to practice law. Leo didn't want to naturally, but he agreed to the terms. That night Mark returned and took the bag full of bills from Leo. That was the last time they would see the old attorney.

Joe wasn't aware of how deep Gina had positioned herself on the small – town political ladder. Gina and Mark had even used her affairs against the policemen and detectives that she had been carrying on with. Black mailing them wasn't easy, in the end they didn't succeed in blackmail, but they did pay large sums of cash out for law enforcement to turn a blind eye. The corruption in Ardmore was horribly rampant. The town officials had dirty hands and there was no one to put them in check. Gina had made friends in high places, she had known that it would all come in handy one day, she hadn't done it all for the future though, she did love the night life and screwing around. It was also a pleasurable experience for her.

They were making profit hand over fist. Joe had been faithful through the entire scheme. Now he was in trouble and hoped that Mark would help bail him out with the police.

Mark had no idea about Gina and Joe or about Joe's secondary job of keeping eyes on him. Mark would have thrown him out on his ass in a heartbeat. Joe was under the impression that Gina and Mark needed him, no they didn't need him they only needed one another. Joe was a pawn on Gina's chess board and he was about to lose his usefulness. He had the idea that he was going to strong arm Gina into forcing Mark's hand and making them get him out of trouble.

"I'm going to tell Mark about us if you don't get me out of trouble!" Joe was talking to Gina in a rushed and irritated tone.

"Why would you do that? All it will do is make him hate you. Besides, he won't believe you." Gina replied coolly.

"Yeah, he will believe me. I know why your nose was busted, he told me all about it. You think you are the only one who knows things around here?"

Gina laughed at Joe, again, he wasn't going to stand for it.

"You know what? You think you are so high and mighty but you ain't and I am going to tell him. I don't care if I go to jail anymore. He knows I would do anything for ya'll and I have! Besides telling him, I am gonna tell the cops about the real house fires, the chop shop, everything! Do you hear me? They are gonna know everything about you two!" Joe was infuriated that Gina had declined to help him get out of his legal trouble. He was letting too many threats escape from his mouth.

"Joe, you need to calm down. I will ask Mark tonight; you really will tell everyone won't you? Damn, I will get Mark to agree to get an attorney and help you out." Gina's gears were turning, she had no intentions of letting Joe near Mark to tell him all of this.

"Thank you, that's all I want. I... I just need some help. I shouldn't go to jail for burning down your house." Joe said slightly mumbling to himself as he left the office.

Gina had already confronted Tim, she had told him explicitly not to involve Joe. Tim had told her that since Joe was the one being looked at by the police then he felt he had done the right thing. He explained that it had been his intention the whole time. If someone was going to take the fall, he was going to make sure it wasn't him. Gina had been mad but quickly let go of that anger when the finger had been pointed at Joe, Tim had been right to do what he had done.

Gina walked out to the garage to make sure Joe wasn't blabbing to Mark. Joe shot her a dirty look, but he didn't open his mouth. The day at the lot was nearly done and Gina asked Mark what he wanted for dinner. He responded that it didn't matter to him, she closed the office an hour later and they were headed home. Mrs. Allen left when they arrived telling her grandson 'bye' and telling the couple she would see them later.

After they had eaten, Gina told Mark she wanted to discuss something very important with him. Mark didn't hold his breath; with Gina it was probably some 'make money quick scheme.' Mark wasn't prepared at all for the bomb shell she was about to drop on him. The conversation was a long one, and grueling. Mark had to make a decision, one that he could never come back from. Gina used her talent of weaving words together to make everything she said sound good and logical.

Mark wasn't prepared for the daunting task before him, but he understood what she was saying, and he knew that she was right. With every word she used, she convinced him further and further that Joe was more than problematic. Gina convinced Mark that Joe had become a liability, she explained the way that Joe was going to tear their little family apart if Mark didn't do something.

By bedtime she had gotten Mark to agree to murder. For the sake of their family, she had repeated those words to Mark like a mantra, she knew that she and her son were his weakness. By telling Mark that Joe had threatened to blow the whistle on their illegal acts if they didn't pay him a ridiculous amount of money, she felt she had clenched Joe's fate.

Fishing

Mark invited Joe on a special fishing trip. Just the guys, they were going to go to the Washita River and take the boat out. Joe agreed, he felt this would be the perfect chance to tell Mark about everything. Joe didn't want to really tell about the affair with Gina, but he would if it meant getting his way. Joe had hated Gina since their trip to Texas and he wanted to hurt her even worse since he was being named as the prime suspect in the couple's latest house fire. Mark couldn't understand why Joe was so elated to be alone with him, he figured Joe surely knew that Gina had told him everything. Maybe he thought he was going to get the payoff he had asked for, Mark thought to himself.

The next day the two men set out for the River, Mark had purchased a new revolver the previous day. He wanted something disposable, his heart raced, and he accumulated a cold sweat knowing what he was going to the river to actually do. Gina was tailing them a few cars back. She had told Mark that she would be the look-out while he committed the atrocity that she so desperately wanted. Gina feared that if Mark found out about anymore affairs that she would be out in the cold. She would sink to any depths of depravity to keep that from happening.

Mark knew of a secluded spot along the Washita, he remained cordial and acted like nothing was amiss. He did his best to hide his shaking hands while working to get the boat into the water. Joe never seemed to notice that Mark was 'off' and tense. Mark did his best to act normal and it was working. Joe just chatted about work, and how he was upset to have been pointed out leaving their house just before the fire. He hinted at wanting help to get out of trouble.

Of course, Mark had already been fed a multitude of lies from Gina, so he figured Joe was working his courage up to present him with the same blackmail. Once the two men had pushed off a few feet from the shore line Gina showed up. She had parked her car nearly a quarter mile away from where the men were and walked the rest of the way to the fishing spot. There, she took a seat behind some overgrown shrubbery, watching and listening to the two men.

Mark glanced at his watch; it was close to time for Gina to have been at her designated place to be lookout. He glanced toward the shore and could barely make out her blonde hair behind the shrubs, he knew where to be looking though. She seen him and stuck her hand up quickly, so he could see her, he gave a small nod of his head. Joe was rambling on about some car they had sitting in the shop and what he thought they should with it.

Mark just mumbled some 'yes's' and 'no's' he was in deep thought about the act he was about to commit. He wasn't the type to kill anyone. Sure, he had anger beyond measure sometimes, but it hadn't been unwarranted anger. The thought of actually taking another human's life was making him sick. Gina's words kept running through his mind 'for his family, for his family.' Mark offered Joe a beer, he figured the guy could use a final drink or two.

Gina sat in her spot growing impatient, she didn't know why Mark didn't just do the thing and be done with it. She had no doubts that she would have already blown his brain's out. She did try to remember that Mark wasn't like her though, not really. He was in her mind, another pawn. One that she would keep and go to any length to keep him. Mark was a driven and passionate man, one that would always have her back. After about an hour she realized what Mark had been doing. He had been giving Joe beer after beer. Joe was tipsy, and she could see it. Gina smiled to herself, she had underestimated Mark's cunning.

"Alright man, you ready to shove off now? I think we've had plenty to drink, don't wanna get caught by no park rangers." Mark said to Joe, looking into the man's bloodshot eyes.

"Oh, yeah man sorry. Here let me grab the rope." Joe tripped when he stood up and fell squarely back on his butt.

"Joe, I'm gonna need you to turn around."

"Ok, why?" Joe looked at Mark with obvious curiosity.

Mark took the revolver from his coat pocket, "Just do it."

Joe's eyes grew wide and he started to cry, he immediately started begging for Mark to not shoot him. Joe kept apologizing for what he had done. He tried to explain to Mark that he hadn't meant no harm by it, that he just wanted out, that he didn't deserve prison time.

"Turn around!" Mark raised his voice this time with the gun still aimed squarely at Joe's head.

Joe turned around and kept weeping, he was crying so hard that Mark's hands began to tremble. Could he really do this? Could he take another man's life?

Mark didn't have to think about it long when Gina appeared with a large rock over her head. She came down with the mini boulder hard striking Joe over the head with it. The man went silent, and blood trickled from his limp body that hung over the boat. The bloody wound on his head ran crimson over his face and into the water. Mark blinked back the shock, he reached out a hand to Gina and helped her into the boat. The men had never waded out more than the few feet from the shore, so they could drink beer before fishing.

"What the fuck Gina?"

"Well someone had to do something! We are going to be here all day, and someone will eventually come by!" Gina raised her shrill, agitated voice at Mark.

"Now, what?" Mark asked her.

"Shoot him!" Gina exclaimed

"I think it's too risky, too loud." Mark said back to her through gritted teeth.

"For fucks sake, pull him out of the boat, we will hold him under." Gina was eerily calm.

Mark hated this, he felt he was going to vomit, but he rolled the unconscious Joe out of the boat and jumped in beside him. Gina hopped out and they began holding Joe's head under. Nothing happened for a second, then the man began to flail about. Trying to hit one of them or both of them, he fought hard he wanted to live. Finally, after a minute or so Mark and Gina seen bubbles rise and felt Joe's body go limp. The man lay dead face down in the water while Mark released him, and Gina held him under just a bit longer to ensure he wasn't getting up.

"What have we done?" Mark whispered more to himself than to her. He had a hot tear slip down his cheek as he pulled the boat back to the ramp and exited the water.

"We did what had to be done. He was going to ruin us." Gina said coldly. She felt nothing but relief, she tried to hide that emotion from Mark but he knew her too well. She made an attempt to look somber but on the inside she was laughing, dancing even. They had snuffed out the life of Joe Lane.

Gina was the worst kind of sick, she was infectious, and her deadly poison had a way of wriggling into the people closest to her. In this case it was Mark. Her charisma was like that of a cult leader, able to talk her flock into doing anything she wanted because, dammit, it was the right thing to do. She was no different than the sickos before her, Ted Bundy, Jeff Dahmer. Hell, if she thought she could make a slave by injecting their head with acid in Dahmer fashion she would have tried it too, she probably would have eaten her victim's heart's while she was at it.

Joe's body was found floating in the Washita River a few days later, Mark's truck had been identified by someone the couple hadn't seen there. The person who seen the truck hadn't witnessed the murder but told the police about the vehicle. Mark and Gina managed to pay off a couple detectives in Ardmore to keep them off the radar. Mark chopped his truck and made it an entirely new vehicle.

By this point he owned two car lots, the body shop but had fazed, out the upholstery shop. With the threat of Joe blabbing his mouth he no longer presented a threat to the couple. Gina knew her affairs with Joe had died with him. There wasn't anyone else who knew about her trysts with Joe. What she didn't know was that Mark had been suspicious of her and Joe and had voiced his concern to one of his family members.

Mark had grown clinically depressed, he tried to raise his spirits by spending as much time with their son as possible. During the following couple of months, he could barely look at Gina. Yet he loved her to no end, he didn't want her to ever leave or stop loving him. He couldn't bear the thought of not having her. She was his first love, his only love and the mother of his child. Now they had such a dark secret between them he felt they would be bonded forever. If something good had come from what they had done that was the good to Mark, they shared something so deep and personal that they would never part.

Mark had recently added restoring classic vehicles to his work load, but he loved it. This helped to keep the nasty nightmares of what they had done to Joe at bay. Mark had always loved classic vehicles and getting to be hands on with them brought a measure of happiness to his otherwise dismal existence. He hadn't recovered from what they had done but he tried to justify it in his mind every day. Gina had gone on with life as if nothing had ever happened. Mark didn't know how she did it but he secretly wished he had her resilience. He never stopped to look at her for what she really was, a remorseless demon who would sink to any depths to get what she wanted or felt she needed.

Running

The couple was on their way to auction a beautiful 1956 fully restored Chevy Bel Air. Mark had done a magnificent job on this car; he had bought it as a scrap heap and turned it back into the beauty it had once been when it rolled off the line. He had it hooked onto a trailer that he was pulling with his work truck. He, Gina and their little boy were all in good spirits that day. Mark had to pull off the highway to get gas, he asked if either of them wanted anything to drink or snack on. Gina said they didn't, and Mark proceeded into the store. He used the restroom and was making himself a fountain drink; he was paying for the gas he had pumped before going into the store. Mark looked out the glass doors in time to see Gina pulling out of the parking lot and back onto the highway! He ran outside to stop her but to no avail.

He grabbed his cell phone and started calling hers. She wouldn't answer. She had their son, his truck, his car, and eighty thousand in cash. They had never deposited the money from blackmailing Leo Whitman. Mark was beyond livid. He didn't know why or where she was going but he was stranded over an hour away from home. He finally reached his brother Mike who had been in Ardmore for a visit the last few days and he came to pick Mark up from the gas station. Mark was silent on the drive back home, Mike tried asking what was going on between him and Gina but Mark didn't feel like discussing it.

Mike eventually let the topic drop and discussed how he and Little Tina had been and how big their daughter was getting. Mark nodded and absent mindedly replied with 'oh yeah?' and 'that's good' he wasn't too interested. Mark listened to Mike the best he could he was in deep thought over what would have caused Gina to take off like she had. What spooked her? He didn't have any answers at the front of his mind. Then Mike said something that got Mark's attention.

"Yeah man, when her and Joe were at our house awhile back, they sure were chummy. I swear if I hadn't known she was your girl I woulda thought she was with that Joe fella. What ever happened to him anyway?"

Mark hung on the 'chummy' part. "What do you mean they were chummy?"

"Oh, ya know, just seemed a little too close. A bit too friendly. He kept touching her back and grabbing her around the waist. She didn't say nothing about it, seemed like she liked it." Mike kept talking.

Mark was seeing red; it was all locking into place. Now he wondered if Joe really had blackmailed them or if Gina was afraid, he would find out that she had been carrying on with Joe as well? He wasn't going to let this slide. He was gonna get his truck, his money, and his son. Mark didn't know much about anything he reckoned but he was finding more and more out every day.

Mark spent the next few days calling her cell phone over and over until she finally answered. He tried to be as patient with her as possible.

"Gina, where are you? I want to see our son. I am trying not to be mad here but you gotta help me out." Mark said with as little tension as possible.

"I'm in Arkansas. I don't know what came over me, I am sorry you have to believe me. We are at my dad's house. I still have the money; I don't know why I ran." Gina replied with a whimpering strain in her voice. Like that of a child in trouble.

"I am coming to get you and the kid. You better be there. I am so sick of this bullshit Gina. You have to get your head on right, we have to do better." Mark really tried to believe in what he was saying.

Gina agreed and Mark made the trip to Arkansas to retrieve her and their son. It was a long drive and he managed to cool off before getting there. As with most people, the immediate anger was over and now he just wanted her and his kid back in the safety of his presence. When he reached her dad's place Gina took Mark outside to talk in private. While they had been apart, she had found another chance to make some quick cash. Mark didn't deny her what she wanted, he never had, and he wasn't going to start now. As mad as he would get at himself for letting her rule over his life, he was powerless to stop it.

Gina explained that there was a truck that had been sitting unsupervised. She wanted to get it across the state line before it was noticed and sell it for a quick few thousand. Mark agreed, he had his classic Bel-Air back and the money they had swindled from the attorney. Why not steal a truck? He just didn't care anymore. They managed to pull it off, of course, Gina drove the work truck that Mark owned, and he took the hot truck. Gina was never one to put herself at risk. Mark decided to bide his time deciding rather bringing up her affair with Joe was even worth it, he had just gotten his family back home and he didn't want her to run again.

For now, he decided to let it ride. There was no bringing Joe back and now he knew that she had wanted him gone for more than one reason. Mark hated the drama that Gina brought into their home, but he decided on the flip side of things, after all, he did have a child that she knew nothing about. He thought he would try to give her this one, because he didn't feel he had been any better. Not only had he lied to Gina to begin with, he had also left Chasity high and dry. He never even claimed his other baby. It was something that would haunt him for the rest of his life, and he knew it.

The New Millennium

Mark and Gina seemed to be getting along normally again. The brothers hadn't seen one another in a while. Mark decided to have Mike and Little Tina down for a visit that would last a couple days. It was getting close to the holidays and he was feeling more festive than he had in years. He wanted to enjoy this season with his family and have a peaceful time with his other brother and his sister, and their mom of course. Gina had never grown to care about Mrs. Allen but that was ok with Mrs. Allen, she loved her grandchild and he loved her, that was good enough.

Mark was a family person and that was something that had always been lost on Gina. She didn't understand a strong family bond. She had little regard to family in general. Gina took care of her child to the best of her ability but outside of that she didn't have any basic instinct except for when it came to caring... for herself. Gina regarded the life of others rather casually. Other people's lives were like playthings to her, she had never been raised any better than that.

Everyone had a fine Christmas that year and Mike and Little Tina along with their daughter stayed until after the new year. The little families had a great time together. The kids played and the adults had drinks and conversation at night. This was the most normal that things had ever been for Mark since being with Gina. He felt so wonderful about how things were turning for the better.

They had managed to stay out of legal trouble, Joe Lane was now a memory, and the affairs had all stopped. Mark felt everything was right with his world. He went into the new year with a new uplifted heart.

The year 2000 had rolled around and everyone was still in one piece. There was no end of the world or y2k. All of the dooms – day predictions had been wrong. However, if they had been looking at Ardmore, they would have been correct in their assumption of impending doom. Gina was making damn sure of that. She wasn't going to stop until she had everything she wanted. Mark still wouldn't marry her, and she felt loathing toward him for it. Mark was completely hers, completely enraptured by her but he wouldn't marry her. He never gave an explanation as to why he didn't want to be married but in the back of his mind it was because he knew if he married her then he would lose any ounce of control that he felt like he had left.

Business was doing good, their finances were straight for the first time in a long time, Gina and Mark had managed to finally settle down and act like a nuclear family. Gina made occasional trips to Dallas to bring back parts for the car lot, and outside of that they were almost always together. Tim had always kept his mouth closed about how the car lots had been used to run illegal operations out of, he was just there for the fat paydays he received for all of his work. Just for security Gina would slip him a little extra money most weeks. This was a fair arrangement to Tim, so he kept quiet. He didn't really care what they did as long as he didn't get caught.

2000 was seemingly a great year. A new baby was on the way, Gina had told Mark the happy news that October of 2000. They found out they were going to be having a perfect little baby girl this time! Mark was over the moon. The first year of the new millennium gave rise to wonderful and happy times. He was going to have his son and now a daughter, he couldn't ask for more and he felt life was going to get better from here. Yes, 2000 had been a great year.

The Long Winter

The year 2000 soon faded into 2001, Gina was up to something again, Mark knew it he could feel it with every fiber of his being. He talked to his brothers about how he was feeling. Mike tried to reassure him that 'Gina's pregnant man, how is she going to be out on the town?' Mike did well at playing the mediator. James however, he had grown up with Gina being a (more or less) permanent fixture throughout his childhood and now late teenage hood.

James didn't care for Gina; he could see what she was. James did his best to comfort his brother, but Mark wasn't always consolable. Now was one of those times, Mark had such heavy suspicions of her that he couldn't be reasoned with. Mark wasn't treating Gina any different, but he was planning to catch her doing something. What kind of woman who is five months pregnant sneaks out in the middle of the night? No, he was going to put a stop to this.

Much to his surprise Gina announced that she was going to Madill to visit with her mom and grandma the following day. It was February 7th, 2001. Mark was fine with that; he knew it would give him time to do some much – needed work at the car lot. He was surprised though because Gina never went to see her family, not even after the terminal cancer diagnosis her mother had received a few months prior. When he really began to think about it, her visit was strange and sudden. Mark felt an uneasiness welling up inside him. He tried to shake it off and work, the day dragged on and he never heard from Gina. By evening he started trying to reach her cell phone. She wouldn't answer and he was getting increasingly worried. Finally, after many calls to her cell he decided to call her mother's land line. Same thing, no answer, then when he had decided this would be his last call before showing up there Gina's mother answered.

"Hello?" the old lady said with a biting edge in her voice.

"I need to talk to Gina, is she still there?"

"Yes, she is but she doesn't want to speak to you. She said she isn't coming back home. So, you can stop calling!" Gina's mother said rudely.

Mark could hear some shuffling and what sounded like a bit of arguing from the other end. He could hear it clearly after a moment. It was Gina telling her mother to give her the phone. Gina got on the line after a few moments,

"Stop calling Mark. I am not coming back, and I mean it this time. We are over, I am done and moving on with my life." Gina spat into the other end of the line.

"Gina, what in God's name are you doing now? Why do you have to always be like this? What did I not do this time?" Mark asked hotly.

"That's just it Mark, you never do anything. You always leave me to do the hard work, the heavy lifting. You won't marry me so what's the point of even being together?!"

Mark stood with the phone to his ear, he had no idea what she was rambling about. He had always given in to her, he had always forgiven her when she had messed around. Hell, he was the one who kept her out of prison. He had literally done every despicable thing that she had asked of him. He couldn't fathom what this was all about.

"Gina… this is crazy. You have no reason to be doing this to our family. We are going to be having another baby and this is how you want things?" When she slammed the phone down, Mark tried his best to control his temper. He hung up the phone and let it go for the moment.

He paced around trying his level best to keep busy and give her time to change her mind. He called again on the 9th of February. It was the same conversation rehashed, she wasn't giving in. Gina did what she was best at, making him feel completely irrational.

"Oh, and one thing you didn't know, *I fucked Derek. Over and over again.* Tell him I said 'hi' next time you guys hang out." Gina was laughing now.

Mark's mind went black, from there he slammed the phone down, climbed in his truck and took off to Madill. Derek was the owner of the competing car lot in town, and Mark's friend. A very good friend. Mark's mind flashed back to listening to the phone recordings, it had been Derek. Mark had let it slide under his radar because his mind wouldn't allow him to believe his *friend* would do that to him. In a single moment Mark realized he had no friends; Gina had completely cut him out of his own life. She had taken everything from him.

Mark reached Madill a half hour later, there was a Sheriff's car sitting in the driveway. The officer approached Mark and informed him that he wasn't allowed on the property. The officer proceeded to tell Mark that Gina was inside the house writing a testimony against him and the criminal acts that he had committed. Mark felt rage then, all the wrath of Hell itself was sitting on his shoulders. He told the Officer that if he didn't let him speak to Gina that many would die that night. The Officer ignored his warning and made him leave. Mark pulled out of the driveway, and in his blinding, hate fueled mind he headed back to Ardmore. Mark was a man of his word; someone was going to die that night.

He sped back to his house, taking his pistol and a shotgun he headed toward Derek's house. Derek was a married man with children, but now in Mark's view he was the enemy, Mark had trusted him completely and he and Gina had made him look the fool. No more, Mark was no longer able to think logically or try to rationalize what he was feeling.

Too many years of her cheating and dragging him into unwanted situations had left their scars. Now he was blanketed in the primordial blackness, no human eyes can see through this blackness, no human heart can find reason in the starkness of the tomb that it becomes locked in. Mark Allen had finally been completely broken by the one person he cherished above all others.

<u>Shots in Ardmore</u>

Mark crept his truck onto the street where Derek lived. Derek's vehicle wasn't there. It was still late evening, under the cover of dark Mark parked his truck down the street from the house. He didn't want Derek to see him immediately. Mark sat there for less than thirty minutes, he thought that maybe he was calming down. He was digesting what he was planning to do to Derek. Mark sat there in the dark, the streetlight letting off an amber glow, he had nearly talked himself out of going through with it. In a turn events he seen Derek pulling up the road behind him, the man pulled his own truck into his driveway. Derek glanced up the street and by chance he could see Mark's truck. Mark was watching him from his side mirror as he approached him. Mark had his window down and could hear Derek calling out 'hey buddy!'

Mark's hand moved to the gun in his waistband, seeing Derek's face was too much. He hadn't calmed down at all, rather his mind had gone into a lull. Upon seeing Derek, his heart raced ten times faster than it should have, he broke into a sweat and all the wrath and blackness was back, gnawing at his fractured mind and heart. Without any more hesitation Mark climbed out of his truck, he pointed the gun directly in Derek's face and let the shot ring out. Mark stood there momentarily, looking at what he had just done. He had taken another man's life, reality was quickly sinking in. Mark jumped in his truck and sped off, Derek's body lay on the street, his face a bloody pulp, legs and arms twitching slightly. His wife came outside to see what the commotion was and began screaming when she seen her husband lying there, faceless and dead in the street.

Mark had another target, Leo Whitman, the scum bag attorney. Leo was another on the long list of people that had blatantly betrayed Mark by using the love of his life like a dime store whore. If he had been thinking properly the thought would have been that she used herself as a whore to get everything she wanted. However, when Mark started past the lawyer's house, he noticed there were police outside. Damn! Someone had already put him in protective custody, Gina must have warned police because they were swarming Leo's house. In flashing lights, something inside Mark finally gave way.

Mark had gone from broken psyche to broken man. He rushed to hide from the police, he didn't know what to do! Everything was happening too fast. He hadn't given himself time to let the reality of his actions sink in. He had taken a life in cold blood and now he was alone, and scared. Mark was on the edge; he did the only thing he knew to do. He hid his vehicle off one of the four Ardmore exits, down in a deep brush and called his mother.

Mrs. Allen called her youngest son James after speaking to Mark. He was just getting off work and the desperation in his mother's voice was frightening. She wouldn't say what had happened over the phone, but she urged him to get to her house. When James arrived, Mike was there too. He knew something was very wrong, Mike would never be in Ardmore this time of night for no reason. Looking from his mom to his brother, James's stomach knotted up in anticipation of the bad news he knew he was about to receive.

James, Mark's baby brother was now nineteen. He knew far more about Mark and Gina's situation than most. Mark had confided in his little brother over the years, just here and there. James had never liked Gina; he had always been able to see through her façade. From the moment he had laid eyes on her at nine years old he knew she was bad. Kids are good at picking up on things like that.

Of course, she had proved his initial reaction to her was not unwarranted. James had been his brother's secret holder for many years now. Mark had always been his idol, he had wanted to be just like Mark when he grew up, but he was old enough now to understand that he couldn't be like his brother and live a normal life. It never changed the way James felt about his big brother though.

Walking into the room where his mom was on the phone with Mark, James asked to talk to his brother. Mike and Mrs. Allen were having a hard time making heads or tails out of what Mark was trying to tell them. James listened carefully as Mark recalled the events of the earlier evening. Mark didn't mention that he had shot Derek. He was speaking in waves of words that dripped with fear and desperation.

James felt the urgency that Mark was conveying and now he was talking about killing himself. It took mere moments for his brotherly instinct to kick in. James got Mark's location and told him not to leave that spot, he was coming to get him, they would figure it out. James started racing to the location of the exit that Mark disclosed. Leaving Mike behind, James was working on pure adrenaline.

James had to make himself slow his car down, he realized he had been speeding and knew that he didn't need to draw any attention to himself. His adrenaline was pumping, and he didn't know exactly what he was going to do once he had reached Mark. All James knew was that his big brother was sitting off exit 24 and he sounded like a man sitting in a boat that was being tossed by a hurricane.

James wasn't going to let his brother hurt himself and from what he could make out during Mark's rant, he knew Gina was at the bottom of this mess. James had never heard Mark sound fearful, urgent or weak. This is what spurred James to get to his brother quickly, the big brother he adored had only ever showed himself to be strong, and seemingly unbreakable. When James heard the crack in his brother's bravado… he knew without hesitation that Mark was truly on the edge.

James's Plan

The sun had dipped behind the horizon a couple hours before Mark's ominous phone call. James looked out the windshield of his car, the passing headlights seemed to pass him at warp speed. He wasn't speeding now but his brain was going full force. James was already trying to figure out what would best help his brother, but he was unaware of the murder. Any plan that he could have settled on was about to torn from his mind when he reached Mark.

James pulled off Exit 24 Oswald Rd and pulled onto the side of the road. He didn't see Mark immediately; he had hidden his truck deeply into the overgrowth that had taken over the side of the road at the exit. Mark finally emerged when he was sure it was James sitting at the exit. He wasn't ready to take any chances. Mark realizing it was James started toward him. James had never seen his brother look scared before, the expression on his face was that of purest fear. James was shaken at his brother's demeanor. In all of his life James had never seen his brother like this. Mark was holding the pistol and the shotgun; James became too aware that there was more going on than just him being angry with Gina and threatening suicide.

"Where is the bronco? And why are you packing guns?" James asked with shock in his voice.

"I did something, it's really bad, I don't know what to do!" Mark replied with that same urgency.

"What did you do?" James asked, with anxiety beginning to grip him.

"I... shot Derek. I killed him."

"What? You did what?" James felt the same alertness he had felt earlier. "Why the fuck did you do that? No, you know what, wait, get the bronco and follow me, we have to get off the roads, NOW." James ordered Mark to get his ass in gear. Mark listened to his little brother, he pulled the truck back onto the road, following James.

Mark wasn't sure where he was following James to, but he wasn't really giving it much thought. All Mark could see in his mind was the body of Derek, the pulp that had once been his face. Deep remorse began to grip Mark. Joe's death had been something he and Gina had done together; he wasn't alone in that act. He had always felt he had someone to share the guilt and remorse for that murder. Mark now knew that there was no way that Gina could have ever felt remorse for what she had caused on that day. He wondered if she knew he would respond this way, had it been her plan to drive him to something like this? Looking ahead at James's taillights he noticed the blinker come on, they turned into an RV park.

James stopped his car away from nearby campers and close to a heavily wooded area. He knew his car wouldn't make it into the wooded area, so he hopped out and instructed Mark that they were going to push the bronco into the woods. They pushed with great effort to get the heavy vehicle far enough into the woods that it wouldn't be noticed anytime soon. The brothers then climbed back into James's car and pulled onto the road. James was driving aimlessly while Mark explained what had happened.

"She's turning over on me. The house fires, the chop shop, all of it. I went to Madill to see her but there was a cop there already. He told me she was in the house writing a testimony against me. Before that she told me about her and Derek. Man, I lost it. I don't know what I was thinking but I lost it." Mark was explaining to James.

"Dammit Mark, I knew she was a bitch, but she wasn't worth this. We have to get you out of here. I'm not letting you go down for her. She might as well of pulled that trigger." James was trying to find the words to calm his brother.

"No, I did it. I can't blame her for this one. I don't want you involved any more than you already are James. I can't go back to the house; I don't plan on going to prison either…" Mark trailed off.

"Look, I know where we can hide you for a few hours. Just give me some time. I will get you out of here, we can leave together." James at the young age of nineteen had it in his head that he could fix the situation.

James drove to a lake; under the cover of darkness he broke into an empty boathouse. He instructed Mark to stay there and wait on him to return. Mark felt like he was holding off the inevitable, but he did what his brother asked of him. Mark went into the boathouse and waited while James began putting a plan into action. James called his roommate on the way to their place, he told him to be ready he needed his help and he couldn't ask questions.

Kyle was more than willing to help, he trusted James completely they had been buddies for long enough that Kyle didn't see the point in even prying. He didn't force James to answer any questions about his odd request he knew by the look in James's eyes it was important. It was a simple task, go to a hotel and rent a room, bring the key back to James. James paced the house contemplating his next move. He had some ideas, then it hit him like a ton of bricks. He knew what the next step would be.

Mike's ex – wife, Big Tina, she had connections good connections. James had stayed in contact with her over the years and they were still friends. Even after what Mike had pulled with leaving her for her best friend, she was the one James needed now in this time of turmoil. James loaded into the car and once again headed out; he was on his way to find what he hoped would be Mark's salvation. James pulled into Big Tina's driveway and rushed to the door; he was moving at the speed of light but felt like he was in slow motion. His mind was overloaded with saving his brother from whatever fate might befall him.

James knocked on the door to the house with quick succession. Big Tina answered the door surprised to see James standing on her stoop during this time of night. Mark was on the news now though, Big Tina ushered James inside.

"What the hell is going on?" She asked with concern in her voice.

"I need your help; it has to be tonight. You know that guy you told me about? The one who forges documents. I know you don't like knowing what he does ok, but I need help." James said in a flurry.

"What do you need? What are you thinking about trying to do James?" Big Tina asked him with more obvious concern.

They could hear the news program in the background, Big Tina's new husband was plopped on the couch watching the story unfold. The man looked in the kitchen at James with disdain on his face. Big Tina noticed it too, she walked into the living room and told her husband he had better keep his mouth shut. The man said he would, he let her know he wasn't a snitch, but he wanted whatever her and James was doing wrapped up soon. Big Tina told him to shush it and walked back to where James was waiting.

"Is he going to be a problem?" James asked.

"No, he's just being an ass. Anyway, what papers do you need? I'll call him and get a rush put on things."

Big Tina owned a business that had a few illegal immigrants employed. Luckily, she had one that was a pro at forging documents. James had it in his head that he would get forged socials, birth certificates, and drivers – license. He had every intention of taking Mark out of state. Texas was his planned destination until he could get them further. At nineteen James was feeling like a regular 'James Bond.'

Three, Two, One

Mark was sitting in the boathouse when he saw headlights. James got out of his car and told Mark to come on, he had a plan. Mark was quiet now, he had been waiting for a couple hours, thinking, deliberating, and feeling the entirety of what he had done. James was explaining the plan to Mark as he drove him to the hotel. Mark sat listening to his little brother's plans and idea. He would nod and say 'ok' trying to appease James.

Mark had certainly lived a life that he would never have lived if it hadn't been for his love for Gina. She had managed to single handedly ruin him; he had allowed her to turn him into some one that he was never meant to be. These things were turning in his mind when they reached the hotel.

James made sure no one was watching and snuck Mark into the room. When Mark had sat his cell phone on the side table James took it. He told his brother not to be using the phones, it was too dangerous right now. James sat in the room with his brother for a while, waiting for Big Tina to call him with news of the paperwork.

"James, thanks for all you are trying to do for me." Mark said with sadness in his voice.

James looked at Mark and told him that he was welcome, he would do anything for him. James didn't like the dark heavy feeling that was coming from Mark. James felt like his brother was giving up, he reassured him that they were going to get out of there and put this behind them.

"I need you to leave and not come back. If you get caught helping me, tell them I kidnapped you." Mark instructed his brother.

"I would never do that! I am not going to get caught and I am NOT going to tell them you kidnapped me." James retorted.

"You are my little brother, and I want you to know that I have always accepted you for who you are." Mark said to James with love in his voice.

James felt his chest tighten, Mark didn't talk like this, with everything happening around them it felt unnatural how calm Mark was now. James knew in his heart that he might not see his brother again. At Mark's request James left, he went back to his mom's house under no certain terms. James was exhausted and hated leaving Mark there alone. He tried to sleep for a few hours, it was now approaching four a.m. on February 10th, 2001.

James woke to the ringing of his cell phone. Thank God it was Big Tina, she had come through with the paperwork. James looked out the window at his mom's and could see unmarked cars surveying the house. He needed to get those papers then back to Mark. He decided to drive as far as Big Tina's house. The police were following him, he could see the unmarked cars following his every turn. He pulled in her drive and went inside; Mark was plastered everywhere now. All the major news outlets, the front page of their local paper... it was a nightmare.

James called his friend Beth, he asked her to meet him at the old 'make out spot' near the high school. Beth had seen the news; she didn't prolong the conversation. She agreed to meet him there and that was all James needed. James called Kyle and asked him for another favor, he needed him to drive to the 'make out spot' to meet Beth. Kyle agreed, James told him to pull around the back, he didn't want the unmarked police cars to see them leaving.

Kyle arrived and James went out the back gate of Big Tina's yard. Looking around with sweat furrowing on his brow, James didn't see any of the familiar police vehicles. He quickly jumped in the passenger seat and ducked down. As they drove Kyle remained silent, he didn't have words of comfort for James, he knew this was a volatile situation. James didn't notice the silence he was watching the rearview mirrors. He noticed as they drove the main stretch of road in Ardmore that they were being tailed by three unmarked vehicles. The drive to meet Beth was going to be a bust if they decided to pull the car over. James couldn't afford to be held up by the cops, he instructed Kyle to try and lose them in the suburban neighborhoods.

Kyle turned onto a side road lined with houses and continued to drive as if nothing was amiss, at last James seen an opening. It would be a difficult strategy but he was hell bent on getting back to Mark. Looking in the rearview mirror neither of the teenagers saw any cops. James told Kyle to slow the vehicle down and without warning he threw himself out. Rolling into a ditch, the breath knocked out of him he got back to his feet as fast as he could and made a mad dash for cover in a nearby house's backyard. From here on, it was going to be a long run to Beth.

James had no choice. He began to sprint through neighbor's yards, and back side roads. His heart hammered begging for a break but James pushed past the burning in his legs and the feeling that his heart was going to explode. He pushed himself as hard as he could, it took between thirty minutes and an hour to reach Beth's vehicle. James felt elation at seeing her sitting there waiting on him as she had promised.

James entered the vehicle and told her where to take him. He needed to get back to Mark with the papers he had been clutching. Beth didn't pry but James explained the situation to her on the way to the hotel. It was a short drive compared to the marathon he had just ran. They had neared the hotel, in front of them James could see the blue and red lights of police cars and… an ambulance.

The Day the Angel Wept

Beth pulled into the parking lot across the street as James and her watched the scene unfolding before them. James's heart and soul cried, for what could he do? He couldn't rush into the commotion in front of him, he didn't shed a tear, not yet. The surrealness of what was taking place before him had him caught in a world of numbness and disbelief. He wasn't sure what had transpired in the few hours he had left his brother. They watched together as the ambulance pulled onto the street. James asked Beth to follow it to the hospital.

On the drive there James held onto the smallest of hopes. He knew that Mark had been in the depths of darkness and remorse. He knew that Mark had been on the edge of a balancing rope, slowly falling. He had done all he could to keep his brother in the smallest sliver of light. Then the thought hit him, he had to tell his mom, Mike and Lisa. Panic started to set in, his heart knew that Mark was gone, yet he hadn't seen for himself yet. As they drove behind the ambulance James made the call to his mom, she left the house immediately and drove to the hospital.

James watched the ambulance pull in at the back of the hospital. His worst fears confirmed. The EMT workers weren't rushing to save a life, they were moving at a normal pace like someone carrying out their daily work duties. Panic turned to a cold piece of ice in the pit of James's stomach as he watched them unload the ambulance. The only thing he could see was his brother's boots.

He watched in disbelief as they unloaded the gurney that carried Mark. James began to cry, his mom, Mike, and sister Lisa hadn't made it to the hospital yet. He felt alone with the totality of Mark's death on his shoulders. James had never felt heartbreak like this in all his life. He still didn't know how his brother had died, he was going to soon find out and it would change his view of this world forever.

When Mrs. Allen arrived, the family went in together, there, they were told that Mark had suffered a self – inflicted gunshot wound to the head. Mark had taken his own life. The news was devastating, the loss itself was devastating but to know that he had died by his own hand because he felt no other way out was utterly gut wrenching. The Allen family lost too much that day. There were more dark days ahead of them that they couldn't have begun to fathom, Gina wasn't done with this family just yet.

Gina showed her ruthless, demented face at Mark's funeral. She came into the church playing the part of a grief – stricken widow to the letter. Her false tears poured, and she made a scene of herself. Gina could never stop being the center of attention. Holding her pregnant belly, disrupting the service all in the name of attention. Gina was in the process of being escorted out when Mike spoke up. Mike actually argued for her to get to stay, he claimed she had a right to be there. James was shocked that Mike would do this after everything she had brought upon their family. It was odd and didn't go unnoticed by James.

There was much that happened between the day they lost Mark and the day they laid him to rest. While the family was in a grief fueled daze, Gina had taken full advantage. She had gathered her friends and rented a giant U-Haul, she emptied the house she, Mark and their son shared. Gina took the things that she knew would add pain to the family's loss, photos of Mark, that was one of the biggest (knife to the heart) kind of pain she caused the family. Gina didn't offer to share any family photos she took every last one for spite. She had her friends strip the house of anything valuable, right down to light fixtures.

Gina and her friends left the house in shambles, tearing through it like a flock of vultures. When James had gotten around to inspecting the home, he found an empty shell with his brother's clothing strewn about the floor. Even in his death Gina still insisted on disrespecting Mark and his family. There was nothing but emptiness where Mark had been. Two families had men taken from them that day in Ardmore, both victims of Gina's twisted appetite for attention, money, and pure selfishness. February 10th ,2001 would be a day that rocked the town of Ardmore for years to come.

Dishonor

Mike Allen, older brother to James and younger brother to Mark. Mike was doing the unthinkable, he was helping Gina systematically wipe out Mark's estate. He told his family that it was her 'right' to do what she pleased with Mark's belongings. However, this was simply not true, they had never married and nothing Mark owned was in Gina's name. It was, by all intents and purposes, thievery. Gina had taken to using the Allen last name, and it was another slap to the face of Mark's family. Mike defended her all the time though; he had taken to being… her protector of sorts.

James his mom and sister Lisa had to resort to tying Mark's assets in probate court. It didn't do much good. The only thing that Gina couldn't touch was the house. The house they originally bought when they first moved to Ardmore. Mrs. Allen was able to keep a hold of Mark's house. It was one of the few things she had left, Gina had taken nearly everything. With Mike helping her it wasn't nearly as difficult for her as it would have been.

James and the rest of the family questioned Mike's motives for helping her, but he maintained that as the mother of Mark's child she deserved to do what she wanted. It wasn't a matter of what Gina deserved, no one knew it, but Mark had left a will he exclusively stated that Gina was to receive nothing that had been his, which was… everything. He wanted his belongings to be liquidated and put in a trust for his son. He had also specified that the house go to his mother. The court did take the will into consideration, the house was the only thing that had been safe from Gina. The Allen's went as far as requesting a paternity test, considering she had been with Derek they only felt it right to know if Mark was the biological father, again the justice system failed. Gina was not made to submit to testing. Mike overruled the family as the executor of the estate.

Mike was travelling between Dallas and Ardmore. His wife Little Tina and their daughter were in Dallas, he would come to Ardmore for visits even though he and his family were on the rocks for the time being. Mike knew his family was disappointed in his actions, but he didn't feel wrong for having helped Gina take everything. Gina had managed to reel him in years before, Mike hadn't been around as much to see the monster she was. It was difficult for him to comprehend that she was the ultimate reason Mark died. Mike tried to see the best in her and it wasn't hard when that was all she was showing him. Gina was able to attract pity much like how honey attracts bees.

When the bulk of Mark's affairs had been dealt with Mike began to stay in Dallas more often, like he always had. It was during this time that the full weight of his brother's death finally hit him like a pile of bricks. Mike became depressed, he now needed someone to be there for him. Little Tina had kept on with life as if nothing happened, she had never liked Mark and she never had given a substantial reason for her disdain toward him. So, Mike was left to grieve his brother's death on his own. When his family had been in the throes of the same grief, he had kept himself busy with Gina and now that he wasn't needed, all of his emotions had come home to roost.

It was during this time period that he started feeling resentment toward Little Tina. She never offered him a drop of comfort, she didn't care that Mark was dead and she didn't feel she should comfort her husband over something that didn't directly affect her. She kept busy with work and their daughter, but she never made any time for Mike, it was as if she was going out of her way to not comfort her husband. The isolation started to take a toll on Mike. Mark passed in February by May Mike was staying more and more in Ardmore. He didn't want to, but he didn't want to stay where he felt unwanted either.

By May, Mike was a permanent fixture back in Ardmore, he and Little Tina decided to take a break. They weren't discussing divorce but things between them had grown sour. He needed her and she wouldn't give herself to him, he couldn't understand why and after a few months of being rebuked by his wife he decided they needed to spend time apart. Little Tina agreed, Mike would still see their daughter, but they were going to work on their marriage with distance between them. On a deeper level both of them knew it wasn't a good idea to attempt to fix marital issues while being apart. However, that is how they decided to work out their differences.

James and the rest of his family were still deeply grieving the loss of Mark. Mike being in town on a full – time basis was strange after all these years and despite how much his family loved him Mike wasn't in the best position with them. James had grown curious of Mike; it had begun at Mark's funeral when he had spoken against Gina being removed. Then it spiked when Mike helped Gina drain everything dry.

There was still thick air between them all. Even with that they all tried their best to just…love one another and let it go as much as they could for the time being. The family was exhausted with hurt and they weren't going to disown Mike over what he had done. He was still an Allen, son, brother, and a dad.

Jess

    Mike packed his clothes and made his appearance back in Ardmore for the first time in years. Catching up with old friends was a good way for him to get his mind off things every once in a while. He and Gina remained friends, he didn't advertise that to his family though. Mike tried to maintain a normalcy in his life, the loss of Mark had weighed on him far greater than anyone could have imagined. Even when helping Gina do what he felt was right, the fact that his family had been disappointed in him made him feel like shit. Mike was a man that did what he felt driven to do and being in Gina's corner had been something he felt was right.

    During the scorching heat of the Oklahoma summer he would go to the lake with his old running buddies when they had a party going. It was at one of these parties he ran across Jess. Jess had been friends with the Allen brothers when they had been kids but now, she was not a kid. Mike couldn't help but notice how beautiful she had become. He wasn't one to be shy, so he approached her, she squealed in delight when she seen him. Mike's heart did a flip in his chest, it had been so long since a woman had been happy to see him. Jess slung her arms around his neck, and they embraced in a hug. Both of them were grinning ear to ear, it was a sweet reunion.

    "Oh my god Mike! How have you been?" Jess asked in a voice an octave higher than normal.

"Ah, I've alright I guess, how about you girl?" Mike asked still smiling.

"I've been great, just working and hanging out with these clowns!" Jess responded looking over her shoulder at the group of people around the bonfire.

"That's good to hear. I'm back in town while me and the wife work on…differences."

"Oh, I'm sorry, I'm sorry about Mark too. I couldn't believe it." Jess said with sincerity.

"Well, we are all still shocked. I mean no one would have ever thought something like that would happen. Anyway, I would offer you a beer, but I see you already have one." Mike said changing the subject, trying to steer the conversation away from the tragedy.

"Yeah but I'll take another one! This one's about gone." Jess responded then finished the last of the can off.

The two visited for a couple hours, she told him what her life had been like the last several years and he did the same. He wasn't going to cry on her shoulder about Little Tina though, in this moment it was just him and Jess. Mike wasn't one to whine about his personal issues. Jess had an effect on him, the effect of making him forget his problems in the here and now. He was appreciative of the time they were spending together now at the lake.

Mike and Jess said their goodbye's eventually and exchanged numbers. She was single and he was (in his mind) practically single. Mike wanted to stay in touch with Jess, and that wasn't lost on Jess. She wanted to spend time with him just as much. Jess had always adored him and Mark but now it was different. Jess felt a strong attraction toward Mike, much the same as he felt toward her.

Mike hadn't noticed her, but Gina was there, hugely pregnant. She wasn't in their immediate group of people, down the shore though, she could see Mike and Jess talking. Gina wasn't happy with what she was seeing. In her mind Mike was hers just like anyone else who showed her kindness. Gina needed to feel like the top dog, the one in supreme control. Instead of making her presence known to Mike, she pulled her phone out and made a call.

Doppelganger

It didn't take long before Mike and Jess were falling for each other. Mike hadn't felt the tender touch of a woman in a long time. Little Tina had rejected his touch for a long time before they had finally decided to take a break. Now he was face to face with Jess and she was everything he wanted. Their affair was a whirlwind, it had begun before either of them had time to think about it. Jess knew that he was married but she didn't care, she figured he would divorce Little Tina and be hers. Mike wasn't thinking of the woman he had left in Dallas either, he was having fun and living in the moment.

They didn't discuss any particulars of their relationship, they both let their free – spirited nature's take over and the rest of the world was temporarily on hold. They both felt the adrenaline that comes along with doing something forbidden, it was intoxicating. After a couple weeks into May they didn't bother to hide the bond they shared from their friends, among those friends Gina was included.

Mike remained friends with Gina throughout everything. He didn't hide Jess from her, he didn't see the point. She had never shown him a reason to not trust her. He wasn't ready for the entire town to know about him and Jess, he wanted to do things on his own terms. Mike felt his secrets were safe with Gina.

James knew of the affair too, but he wouldn't reveal his brother's secrets. James felt that what people did was their own business was just that. It was how he had been raised, to mind your own business. The Allen siblings had all been taught that lesson. James had never divulged the things he had known about Mark, and he wasn't going to do it now to Mike. James had his own feelings about how Mike had helped Gina, but he was working to let it go. He had lost one brother and he didn't want to lose another one because he couldn't let go of emotional baggage. Mike confided to his brother about the affair and James listened, being his brothers safe place.

May had not yet ended and Gina was swollen to the point of popping. She was going to have her and Mark's baby girl any day now. Mrs. Allen and the rest of the family had decided rather the baby was biologically Mark's didn't matter. He had claimed the baby, and they knew Gina would give this child the Allen last name, even if she were Derek's. They wanted to see Gina and Mark's children and be a part of their lives, but Gina had become impossible to deal with on the subject.

The day came when Gina gave birth to a wonderful baby girl. She nor her family notified Mark's family. James, Mrs. Allen, or Lisa were allowed to visit and see the new addition. When they heard it through the grape vine that Gina had given birth they were harshly told to stay away. Oddly, Gina reached out to Mike, Mike went to see the baby girl and kept the secret away from his family.

They remained in the dark on this secret, Mike looked at the child with adoration. The baby was perfect, he hoped that Gina would change her mind and let his family be a part of her life, but she never would. Gina made it abundantly clear that Mark's family was to have nothing to do with either of her children. Never mind that they were also Mark's children. Gina had put her own mother in nasty predicament, why would she care about Mark's family? The thought to her was laughable.

When Gina's mom had been diagnosed with terminal cancer she had asked to live with Gina and Mark. Gina had told her mom that she could live in their backyard, in a camper under the rule that she babysat her son. That was the mentality of the woman that now had control over everything that had been and still was Mark Allen's. Mike still went along with the choices Gina made regarding his own family. It was lost on everyone who found out that he betrayed them for the likes of someone like her.

It was hard for Mark's family to cope with not being allowed to see the children. They tried but at every turn they were shut down. Because Mark had never married Gina there was no law that could force her to let them be in their lives. It was another victory for Gina every time she got to hurt Mrs. Allen in some way.

Mike acted oblivious to everything and kept seeing Jess, she was his comfort now. He had all but abandoned his family by this point. Mike was no longer the person that James had once known. James knew his brothers better than anyone and Mike's actions were lost on him. None of them could wrap their minds around his standoffish and odd nature. Mike had always been an upbeat person when he did come down from Dallas, and he shared in his family's woes and their good times. Mike had become someone else completely.

The Last Trip to the Lake

It had been nearly a month since Gina had the baby, she was back in full swing with the party crowd. It was humid as Hell and over a hundred degrees out. Mike, Jess, Gina and an assortment of local friends were down at the lake, per their usual party spot during the summer months. They had all packed into Mark's old camper that was now Gina's and decided to make a weekend of it. Jess and Mike were together, much to Gina's disdain. Mike was trying to not pay her much attention. He could feel the cold stares coming from her eyes.

Mike hadn't checked in with Little Tina in several days and he didn't plan to either. He was having fun, cutting loose, and getting to be with Jess. He was happy for a change; he missed his daughter though. His sweet little four – year - old daughter. Mike knew he would have to go back to Dallas at some point and see the wife and child he left there. He wasn't sure if his marriage was going to work or not, but he didn't show his worry to anyone.

Inside him raged an internal battle, he loved Little Tina, he truly did but she made him feel unimportant. That wasn't his main concern though, his biggest concern was his daughter. The guilt of not having seen her in a month was taking its toll on him. He tried to push these thoughts away and concentrate on Jess and the party he was at.

The group spent the night at the lake, wiped out and drunk. Some people were piled in the camper others were under the stars. Mike opted for him and Jess to sleep outdoors, he didn't want to be in Gina's direct line of sight. He had enough of feeling her eye daggers for one day. Mike wondered why she was acting so peculiar, but he didn't bother asking her. He knew that much about Gina, she would just dismiss whatever he said with a flick of her hand. She would make him feel as if he were imagining things, he didn't care for that aspect of Gina's personality.

The night was muggy, and miserable for everyone not in the camper. Mike and Jess were making the most of it though. They slipped back in the lake for a late night swim, the water wasn't very refreshing due to the extreme Oklahoma heat, it felt more like warm bath water. Even so, it was wet and was better than lying on the sleeping bags. Jess with her arms wrapped around Mike asked him a question...

"Do you think you will go back to Dallas and work on things with your wife?"

"I don't know, she has our kid and that does make a difference in things. She doesn't seem too eager for me to rush back." Mike answered.

"Well, if you don't work things out then do you think we could give it a try?" Jess asked softly.

"Yes, why wouldn't we? We are already together; I wouldn't leave you if me and her don't work out." Mike said with a chuckle.

The two spent the rest of the night swimming in the dark, drinking cold beer, and not thinking about tomorrow. They finally fell asleep after enough drinks; the Oklahoma heat was merciless.

The next day everyone was back in the full swing of swimming and grilling hot dogs over the fire they had built. No one wanted to stay near the flames too long, the good times ensued but Mike kept catching Gina looking at him again. It was beginning to get on his nerves, if she wanted to talk, he didn't know why she didn't approach him. It was so bad that he went out of his way to make sure where ever he was that she wasn't there.

Music was blaring, people were swimming, hot dogs on sticks, beer, who could ask for more summer fun than that? Mike's uneasiness was fading with each beer. Him and Jess were sitting in a couple lawn chairs near the camper and Gina was in the water, finally, peace. Mike wasn't really thinking of much other than the present moment when he could feel his phone vibrate in his pocket. Taking it out the number belonged to his neighbor in Dallas. Alarmed he answered the phone,

"Hello"

"Heya Mike, I didn't know you and Tina were moving."

"What? We aren't moving." Mike responded perplexed.

"Oh? Well, there's a truck here and Tina's outside helping pack it up. Looks like they are almost done. Sorry if I stepped into something here." The neighbor said feeling extremely awkward now.

"No, you didn't, thank ya, bye." Mike hung up the phone. Without a goodbye or see ya later he got in his truck and drove for Dallas.

Watching Mike tear out of the lake area Gina smirked and Jess was in complete shock. Jess had no idea what was happening and more over she couldn't believe he had just left her there.

Mike didn't know what the hell was going on, but he called Little Tina repeatedly on his way back to their home. Naturally, she didn't answer. He knew what she was doing, and by god his mind was made up in that moment. Mike did not want to lose his wife, something changed, snapped into place like a puzzle piece. He knew he had been in Ardmore doing her wrong but now that the reality that he could lose her sunk in, he didn't want it to happen.

Back to Dallas

Mike put his foot down on the gas, speeding back to Dallas. He hoped she would still be at the house when he arrived. Mike made record time getting there but Little Tina and their daughter were gone. The house lay bare, much the way they had left Mark's home. He called his family in Ardmore and let them know he was in Dallas and what was going on. Now he wanted to find his wife and fix everything.

It was going to be a long wait until he heard from Little Tina, Mike had gotten back to their house on a Sunday night and it would be nearly a week of calling and asking everyone where she had gone. Little Tina had absolutely refused to answer any of his calls. He waited though; he knew she couldn't hold out forever. Finally, it was on Friday of the following week that he was able to catch her at work.

She talked to him and agreed to meet. Mikes worst fear was now a reality though, she knew about Jess. Little Tina told him over the phone that Gina had called her in May, she had told Little Tina she suspected the affair then. It wasn't until Gina had the baby that she had reached out to her again and confirmed the affair. Mike was livid with Gina, but he couldn't deny what he had done. He just wanted the chance to make things right with his wife.

Mike, Little Tina and their daughter met at restaurant that evening, they hadn't sat down as a family in quiet sometime. It felt good, and Mike hoped against hope his wife would forgive him. Things seemed to be going really well, they had a pleasant dinner and Little Tina even invited him to stay at the hotel that she and their daughter had been staying at. Mike couldn't have been happier. He still felt a burning anger toward Gina, but he felt so lucky that his wife was willing to work on his trespasses.

The family made their way to the hotel and spent time catching up. The parents weren't going to discuss their issues in front of their small daughter. They watched movies and chatted instead, trying to ignore the elephant in the room. Elephant or not Mike and Little Tina snuggled together, before long Mike was in a deep slumber. While he was drifting further into sleep Little Tina lay behind him with her eyes open, holding him but her eyes fixed on his back to watch his breathing. When it was slow and shallow, she removed herself from bed.

Quietly she unplugged the phone from the wall and hooked it into the jack in the bathroom, then she put boxes of belongings she had brought with her and stacked them in front of the hotel door. She locked herself and their daughter in the bathroom and called the police. She urged them to get there quickly that she and the child had been kidnapped! Her story was that she waited for him to sleep and snuck her and their daughter into the bathroom, she stated that he had locked and barricaded the door to keep them locked in.

Mike woke to the door being knocked down and guns aimed at him! He was utterly confused as to what was happening. Mike raised his arms and did as the police said. It was during him being cuffed that he heard his wife's voice telling police her story about how he had kidnapped her and their child. Little Tina was acting frantic and crying. Mike told the cops that it was all a lie, she was making it up, but they took him in none the less. Dallas has more than one county and he ended up in Tarrant County Jail. They didn't allow him a phone call immediately, and it was now Saturday in the wee hours of the morning.

Mike's pleas of innocence fell on deaf ears, the police saw what they saw, and it certainly looked suspicious. With Little Tina's accusations and the appearance of the room showing signs that there had been foul play. The police weren't taking any chances on Mike NOT being a deranged and violent spouse. Mike was booked and charged with kidnapping; he couldn't believe she had done this to him. Yes, he had cheated on her in Ardmore but to let him take the fall for a crime he hadn't committed was too much.

When Mike was able to make his phone call, he rang his mom. He didn't know what was going to happen to him yet and the police informed him there would be no bonding out during the weekend. He would have to see the Judge on Monday. Mrs. Allen was full of dread; she asked the officers at the station to put her son on suicide watch. After what she had gone through only four months earlier, she was terrified that she would lose another son. The officers agreed to do this for her under the circumstances.

The weekend was long and strenuous for everyone. Mike stayed in touch with his family, calling them as often as he was allowed. He spoke to James; James tried his best to be reassuring to his brother. However, James couldn't help but notice as the hours passed and each time, he spoke with Mike that Mike's fighting spirit was becoming less and less. He hurt for his brother, but there was nothing to be done until Mike could see the Judge. That Saturday felt like an eternity to Mike. He tried calling Little Tina, but she wouldn't answer.

In a miraculous turn of events Mike was able to reach Little Tina the next morning! It was Sunday morning and a new day had dawned; Little Tina gave Mike the best news he could hope for. She assured him that she was speak to the DA and recant her statements of being kidnapped. She told him that she had thought about things and it wasn't right to have done this to him, she was just angry. Mike felt relief flood his soul, he was going to be free!

After Mike had talked to his wife, he called James to share the amazing news. James was excited to hear that she was going to recant, he couldn't stand the thought of Mike being in jail for something he hadn't done. Mike's spirits had definitely lifted. Monday morning Mike was transported to his arraignment. Little Tina hadn't talked to the DA yet, Mike knew she would come through for him though. The judge did something that no one was ready for, he put a one – million - dollar bond on Mike. The amount was staggering, and completely unexpected.

Mike called James again after the hearing and told his brother the ominous news. James freaked out; this amount of money was insane for a middle - class family. Mike asked his brother to call Little Tina and ask if she had spoken to the DA yet. James agreed, and quickly called her.

When James finally got Little Tina on the phone, she informed him that she had not gone to the DA yet but that she would.

"Why did you do this?" James asked her.

"I don't know why I did it, I just did it." That was her response to this monumental question.

She told James that she would go see the district attorney Wednesday. He didn't fully believe her, but he held on to hope. When Mike and James next talked James told him about the short conversation and what she had said. Mike's hope was still intact though, he knew Little Tina would explain everything. He knew she was just angry with him over the affair and he felt this was her way of punishing him a little longer. James told him they could try to mortgage the house, but Mike said 'no' he didn't want that. In reality, Mark had left enough money to pay the house off, but he and Gina had split the money after Mark's death. There was no way to help him by using the house.

River of Tears

From Monday to Wednesday felt like an eternity to Mike and his family. No one could get in touch with Little Tina to see if she had kept her word of seeing the DA. Mike called James once again, this time he sounded down trodden. He was no longer fooling himself that she was going to be his savior. Mike told James that he needed to tell him something important. James listened as Mike told him something that he had kept hidden for a very long time.

"Gina's baby is an Allen, just not Mark's." Mike said quietly.

The revelation didn't compute with James at first, he asked Mike how could she be an Allen baby if she wasn't Mark's baby? Mike sat on the other end of the call silent, then as if hit by a bus it dawned on James.

"She's your baby?"

James could hear Mike take a deep breath on the other end of the line. There was a moment of silence and Mike continued speaking

"Look, I'm really sorry about helping Gina screw everyone around. That was a mistake on my part."

James sat listening to his brother in an absolute state of shock. Mike didn't offer any details as to when he and Gina had been intimate but from the timing it had to be the end of 2000. James didn't know what to say to his brother, he was lost for words at this turn of events. Even though Mike didn't directly admit to being her father he might as well of been holding a sign stating it above his head. Mike told him it was Gina that had snitched him out too Little Tina about Jess. He figured it was out of jealousy or pure anger. Mike knew he was innocent of kidnapping his wife and daughter but here he lay bare his sins for James to see.

Midnight, just a few hours after speaking to Mike, James's phone rang. It was an 'unknown' number. A female voice, one that James knew all too well was on the other end.

"Your other brother is dead now." It was Gina. She spoke with pleasure in her voice.

She hung up abruptly and left James in a whirlwind of panic. He immediately called the Tarrant County Jail. The officer who answered told him

"Mike Allen is deceased and that is all we can currently release."

James felt his world shattering again, this couldn't be real. This was a nightmare and he would wake up. Only it wasn't a dream, his remaining brother was gone from this world. James couldn't feel anything his body had betrayed him with this news. He was numb, then he was breaking, falling into a void that he wasn't sure he would come back from. When he was able, he went to his mother's and broke the news. Mrs. Allen felt the same as James if not worse, she had lost another child. No mother should have to endure the pain of losing a child, it is an unnatural pain that only a mother can understand. The family wept for the loss of another son and brother.

None of them slept that night, they had to wait until the morning hours of Thursday to get any answers. They didn't know how Mike had died or what happened, they were in the pitch black. When they were able to get answers, they were told the worst possible scenario, suicide. They were met with yet another slap, he was on suicide watch! How did this happen while he was on suicide watch? The police claim that he used his socks to hang himself.

This news didn't make any sense, Mrs. Allen had specifically been told he was in a cell alone and on suicide watch. Mike hadn't been suicidal not openly, and he never showed signs of wanting to die. James told anyone who would listen about the phone call from Gina but again everything fell on deaf ears. This was a gross case of negligence, the Ardmore police failed them and now the Tarrant County Jail was a failure. Neither departments were worthy of saying they had 'justice' in their systems.

Pulling Back the Veil

James tried to reach Little Tina to tell her all that had happened. She had gone off the grid, cutting all communication with Mike's family. James didn't understand why she would do that her husband was dead and she was ignoring his family. She had already been a widow once and now here she was again and had nothing to say? It wasn't normal behavior for such a tragic loss. Given, normalcy is never expected during a time of grief, but she went off the map.

Texas sent Mike's body for a mandatory autopsy since he died in police custody. The coroner's office made quick business of ruling Mike's death as a suicide by hanging. The Allen's were waiting for his body to be returned to Ardmore. They wished to have Oklahoma perform their own autopsy, but Oklahoma said they couldn't do a second autopsy they had reached Little Tina and she forbade it. The family had their fill of being told 'no' it started with Mark's death and now Mike's.

Granted, Mark's death was obviously a suicide but when the family had been pulled in for questioning, everything that they testified regarding Gina, Joe and Tim was dismissed. The ADP had gone as far as to try coaxing James into saying that he had indeed been kidnapped by Mark. Of course, James vehemently denied this because it was not the truth. The Allen's suffered the loss of two family members and the injustice and complete negligence of not only Oklahoma but also Texas.

To make things worse Mike's body was misplaced, lost, for sixteen hours while in transit to the Ardmore funeral home. Nothing was as it seemed anymore. James knew Gina had something to do with Mike's death, but he hadn't figured out how she had done it yet. After the ridiculousness of losing Mike's body and being turned down for a second autopsy James decided to do some investigating of his own. James knew Mike had not committed suicide; it made no sense at all.

After the funeral home had Mike's body ready for viewing mourners came and went throughout the allotted time period. When the last person left James stayed in the room with Mike's body. He couldn't let go of his suspicions that there was more than met the eye here.

Gingerly, he pulled Mike's collar down, he noted the bruising was a thin line, that didn't add up with strangulation by thick tube socks. Next, he noticed the bruising went in a straight line across his neck, had he hung himself the bruising would have been in an upward shape across his neck. This in itself was alarming. James turned his brother's hands over, there was deep bruising on his palms, lastly, he checked under his shirt. James saw puncture wounds on Mike's rib cage.

Mike had been murdered. There was no doubt, the evidence was on his body.

James wasn't letting this go without a fight.

After Mike had been laid to rest James contacted the Tarrant County Jail. He obtained from them that on the night June 11, 2001 there had been another man in custody. Tim, Gina's lapdog. Tim had been placed in the same cell as Mike at some point during that night. The next question was how? James and his family were never given answers as to why Tim was in the same cell however, he had been picked up on a drunk and disorderly charge in the same county. He had been placed in the same cell and he had carried out the murder of Mike Allen.

James later found out from one of Gina's friends that he had heard her saying that she and Little Tina paid the guard on duty to put Tim in the cell with Mike. Unfortunately, the law doesn't regard here say. The case remained ruled as suicide, (Texas had only done a neck up autopsy on Mike.) This was one way that the two women got by on sheer luck.

The Allen's had no choice but to grieve the loss of Mark and Mike Allen.

The brothers will always be dearly loved and missed by their mother and remaining siblings.

One year later Gina and the deputy that Mark encountered the night he went to Madill ended up getting married.

Little Tina remarried an elderly man and is now awaiting his death, she will be three times a black widow.

Tim was given Mark's tow truck and all of the body shop equipment that Mark had incurred during his life.

The children were withheld from their grandma, uncle James and their aunt Lisa.

Justice has never been served.

Mark Allen's last words to his family. This letter was confiscated from the hotel where he died. In his final moments on this planet he remained a family man at heart.

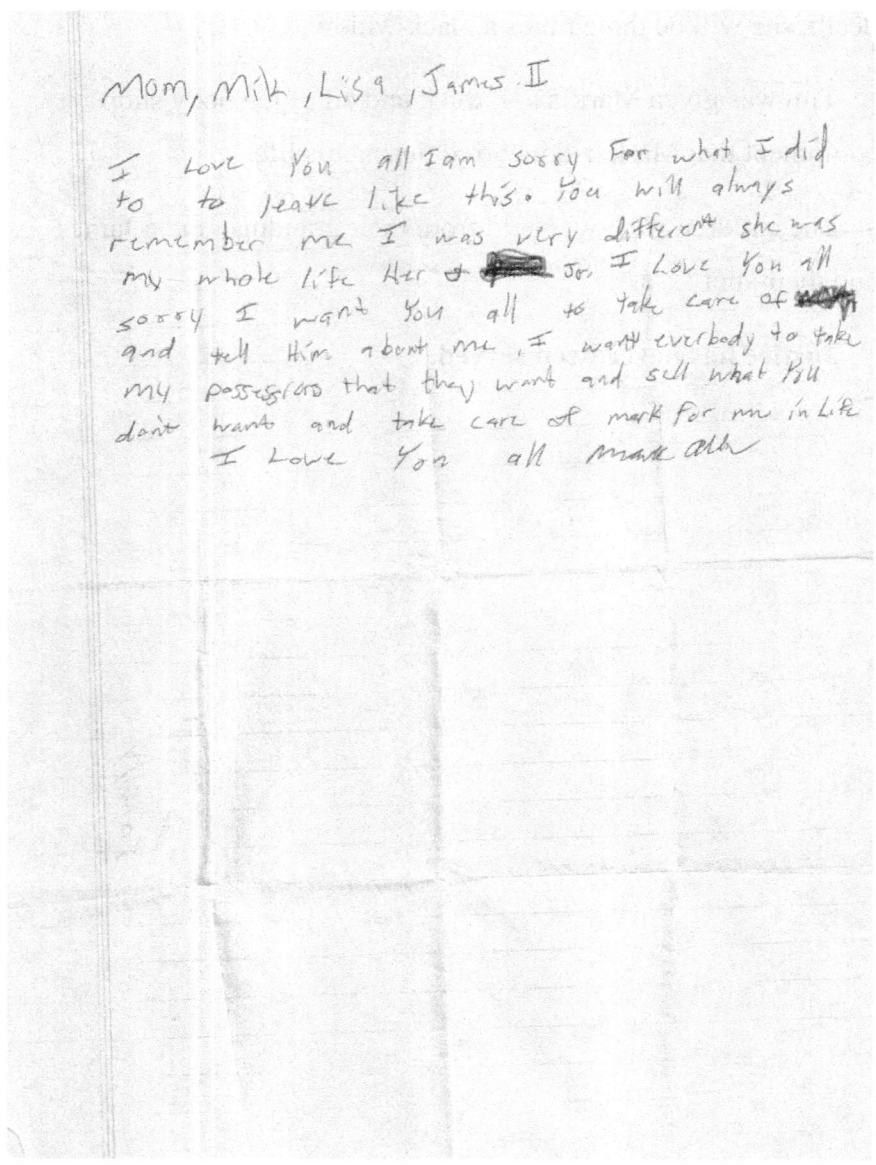

Dedication

Dedicated to the memory of the lives of my older brothers.

Mark Allen and Mike Allen

They may not have led perfect lives but as a child growing into a young man, they were perfect in my eyes. They taught me the value of hard work, and perseverance. As a kid I didn't know what all lay beneath until later in their lives when they confided in me. They taught me to be strong, and I learned what to do and what not to do. They protected me and always made sure I had everything that I needed. I will never forget all of the good times that we shared, all of the goofy things that they would say. One of my favorite memories of Mike was when I was young and he would skip school, he would let me come in his room and he would make up funny stories to tell me. Mark would pick me up from kindergarten and always take me to McDonalds to get a happy meal before he took me to work with him. These are the memories that I hang onto. They left this world far too soon and there isn't a day that goes by where I don't miss them or have at the least a fleeting thought about my brothers. They were loved and they still are loved. No one is innocent in this book, and I know my brothers are finally at rest. Their stories are told, and rather justice is ever served or not, I have given them the only justice that I can and that is to tell their story for what it was, what it is, the truth has been brought to the light of day at long last. You forever live in the hearts of all that knew you.

About the Author

James Allen resides in the Southern United States. James has many interests but primarily he is a business man. He has established many successful businesses in the south. James learned from a young age the meaning of hard work and honesty. When he isn't working, he loves to travel and spend time with his family and dogs. James is a man always working and investing back into the community.

It was his wish to write this book and tell the story of his brothers who cannot tell it themselves. There was so much more to Mike and Mark Allen, the story you read is merely the surface of who these men were and the injustices that were dealt to them. The memory of these men has been threatened by the women who they trusted, despite their trespasses their story deserved to be heard just as any other victims.

To discuss and follow updates regarding this book please follow the link below

https://www.facebook.com/search/top/?q=four%20exits%20to%20hell%20novel

Made in the USA
Monee, IL
09 May 2024